I0611732

They Watch Us Like the Lions

Lindsey Renée Backen

Published by Ever Ink Press, 2024.

While every precaution has been taken in the preparation of this book, the publisher assumes no responsibility for errors or omissions, or for damages resulting from the use of the information contained herein.

THEY WATCH US LIKE THE LIONS

First edition. October 15, 2024.

Copyright © 2024 Lindsey Renée Backen.

ISBN: 978-1944299200

Written by Lindsey Renée Backen.

Table of Contents

The Village

OUT OF ALL THE SMELLS she could resent, it was unfortunate it had turned out to be bacon. Katie frowned as her stomach betrayed her for the third time in five minutes, first quivering, then twisting her gut like a raccoon destroying a trap. She pulled her best dress from the dim closet. Yesterday's efforts of washing, ironing, and trimming the loose threads had only managed to make the gown presentable. The vibrant purple flowers she'd embroidered around the neckline only accentuated their dingy white backdrop.

She avoided the magnifying mirror that sat on her dresser as she stepped into the dress and wrestled with the back buttons. She unbraided her hair, running the wooden comb through its long, light waves, deciding to wear it down and leave behind her red ribbon so its color didn't draw any attention from the bride.

Today was Mallory's day to shine.

She pulled in another steadying breath and hung up her nightdress, tugging the hem so it would hang straight. Practiced a smile. Smoothed her sheets and the quilt made from her family's cast-off clothing. Her favorite squares were from her grandparents' clothes from before the Blackout. Those patches were smooth and soft, created from a material that wasn't from nature. Polyester, her grandmother had called it, but as it had been made in a lab and not grown from the ground, nobody wore it these days or even quite remembered how it had been made.

Summoning every bit of self-control, Katie felt her way along the dim hall, down the stairs where her sister stooped over the coals she'd scraped onto the hearth, flipping the two slices of bacon that sizzled in the cast iron grill.

Katie's stomach growled again, and she pressed her hand against the traitor. She strode past the table and snatched the basket from the counter, speaking in a tight, high pitch. "Morning, Mal. I'll get the eggs."

"I already got them." Still squatting, Mallory turned quickly. "I want to talk to you before Clark gets here."

Katie chewed her lip, then forced her face into something she hoped looked neutral. "About what?"

"I know today is hard for you for lots of reasons," Mallory said. "And I'm sorry we can't keep the farm. I really am. But me and Jeremy talked it over..."

Katie's heart sped, fanning the spark of hope that the wedding was off. Mallory's voice blurred as her mind supplied a host of potential turn of events. "...we really won't mind. You can stay here until it sells, if you want, but then you're welcome to come to our farm if the scholarship doesn't work out."

Pressure expanded like hot air, filling Katie's chest and tightening her throat, summoning the tears she had banished.

"Honey." Mallory's shoulders melted. She stood and took two steps toward Katie.

Katie turned away. Grabbed the back of her father's chair. "Do you really want to marry him? I mean...you're only twenty-one."

"Katie, he's a good man."

"I know, but..." Katie cut herself off, feeling an inner debate between being kind and being truthful. She chose her words carefully, letting them out in a deliberate slowness. "Sometimes I feel like you're just marrying Jeremy because we can't afford to stay here."

"We can't."

"If we have to sell, we could take the money and buy a smaller place," Katie offered.

Mallory blinked, her face pinching like it always did when Katie was trying to explain the laws of thermodynamics or how letters could stand in as placeholders for unknown numbers in a math problem.

"Don't marry him if you don't want to," Katie stated.

Mallory took a deep breath like she was trying to simplify her own thoughts. "Katie..."

The bacon popped in the pan, its edges burning dark. Mallory stooped to retrieve it, scooping both pieces onto a plate. She stood, holding the glistening meat her fiancé had brought as a bribe.

"I *want* to marry him," Mallory said.

"Why?" The one question Katie had forbidden herself to ask, burst out in a wail.

"Because he's kind. And respected." Mallory set the plate onto the table and wiped her palms against her apron. "He's well-established, and he's willing to let you come too. And he makes me happy."

Why? Katie almost asked the question again, dumbfounded at the power the man somehow wielded over her sister. Mallory had always kept near the wall and lots of girls outshone her, but she was sweet and skilled and had access to plenty of other single men who could put a solid roof over her head and would look far better than Jeremy as they did it.

Katie turned away, pulling two of the four eggs from their basket. She cradled them as she crossed to the fireplace, avoiding Mallory's eyes. Sighing, she broke them against the side of the pan, dropping the yokes into the bacon grease.

Mallory took a breath, then spoke from behind her, "Please, try to like Jeremy. For my sake."

"I am trying," Katie said quickly. "I just... I don't see what you see."

"You don't have to. But for the next few years, he's going to be taking care of us, so..." Mallory sighed. "Someday you'll understand. For now, all I want you to know is that we're not going to leave you to fend for yourself."

Clark's boots vibrated the floorboards as he climbed the porch steps, calling through the screen door, "Hello!"

"Good morning, Clark," Mallory said. "Have you eaten today?"

"I have, thank you," Clark answered as he always did, though in his case it was actually true.

Which was good because they'd only cooked two pieces of bacon, and no one had bothered to make a fresh loaf of bread because they wouldn't be here by the end of the week anyway.

Katie sighed, fishing the eggs out of the grease as Clark scraped his boots on the steps and pulled off his cowboy hat before stepping gingerly just inside the door. Katie cut a thick chunk from the heel of the loaf, broke the bacon piece in two and layered the strips onto the bread, ignoring her egg. She walked toward the door, but Clark remained stationed.

His thumb fidgeted with the leather strap on his book bag, his only giveaway as he calmly addressed Mallory. "I want to be at your wedding tonight, and I hope I am. But if I have to skip, I want you to know it's not my choice."

"It's all right, Clark," Mallory said. "With the scholarship letters arriving, this is a big day for you and Katie too. A second celebration would make ours even better."

Clark sucked in a breath so deep he almost looked like a fish. He nodded, then ran his fingers through his dark hair, trying to press down the thick strands that never quite stayed where they should. "It's just..." His eyes flickered miserably to Katie. "My dad already planned...I tried to talk him out of it. I mean, I may...I may not even get the scholarship. And I told him that, so I don't know if he's actually invited anyone, but I think he has, and—"

Katie stopped her greasy fingers just before she clutched her dress. "Wait." She didn't think her heart could sink any lower but found now that it was more than capable. "You're not going to be at the wedding?"

"I hope so," Clark moaned. "I don't want a party, even if I do win the scholarship."

Katie grinned. "I'm pretty sure you're going to win."

"Yeah, but..." Misery broke through his discomfort. His shoulders sloped until he looked like a lost young boy dressed up in a white shirt with starched cuffs that never managed to elevate him to his proper social status as a member of the Blackwell family. "What if I don't?"

Katie shrugged. "Then the whole town will be at Mallory's wedding, and anyone your father did invite will still have a good time."

"And if you do," Mallory added, "it will be okay. Enjoy your party. Jeremy and I would rather have had a smaller wedding anyway and just invited a couple of people. The more people at your party, the less we'll have to host at ours."

The words washed the tension out of the young man's body. He put his hat back onto his head and nodded. "I guess we'll see."

Still summoning both breath and enough poise to speak, Katie asked, "Ready?"

Clark eyed her gown, hesitating. "It's awful muddy out there."

"I'm picking up a new dress at Katherine's shop," she said. "I'll be careful."

Clark's eyebrows traveled a fraction before he tore his gaze from her uneaten sandwich to Mallory, who gripped the back of a chair. He looked like he was going to ask something, and Katie quickly took a bite so her mouth was too full to answer. Clark blinked and opened the screen door. "Let's go."

Katie flashed Mallory a close-lipped smile and snatched the tail of her father's belt that kept her books in a neat, tight stack. It would be empty on her return home, for all books must be relinquished on the final day of school. She ate as quickly as she could, following Clark onto the porch.

Clark glanced down, frowning at the pots that lined the path, where mosquito larvae already wriggled in the rainwater. When they reached the road where the black quarter horse stood, Clark pulled the cow horn flask hanging from his belt and offered it to her.

"It's been raining," Katie said. "You can keep your water."

"It's not raining that much. I can get more when I go home," Clark said. "Besides, my father charges your family twice as much as anyone else in town for the well water. So, technically we owe it to you."

Katie stuffed the last bite of breakfast into her mouth and accepted the cow horn. "What do they charge Jeremy? Are your folks going to raise the price when he marries my sister?"

"They'd better not." Clark flung himself across the horse's bare back, then offered his hand to hoist her up. He grinned. "Although Dad was pretty mad when Jeremy refused him the last side of bacon and then gave it to your sister."

"Oh?" Katie smirked. "That almost makes me want to eat it."

She took his hand, swinging up behind him, relaxing her legs so she didn't give the animal mixed signals. The horse's hooves fell into a familiar rhythm on the road, the clops muffled against packed dirt, occasionally broken by the grind of an asphalt rock.

A light rain wet her face, and she frowned again at the cotton drooping at the edges of the road. No reason to pick the excess. This year, it wasn't the land that had dried up: it was the buyers. She and Mallory had filled their own shelves with bags, sold what they could to the weaver, and left the rest to rot.

Ever since their parents died, the sisters had lived near the poverty line. This year, they'd plunged like Alice down the rabbit hole, falling so far, they'd yet to hit bottom. But the scholarship danced at the back of her mind.

"If the scholarship covers all expenses for college, do you think it covers books, too?"

"I don't know," Clark answered. "I hope so."

"Do you get to keep them, or do you think you'll have to turn them back in for the next student?"

"Books are pretty expensive," Clark said. "You'll probably have to turn them back in. But you could copy it out by hand if you had enough paper."

"I don't think even your dad could afford enough paper to copy an entire book," Katie said.

"He probably could if I got the scholarship," Clark answered, "since he wouldn't have to pay for anything else."

"And you'd copy the entire thing by hand?"

"Sure."

"Yeah right."

"I would," Clark defended. "I think any of us would if we had enough paper. Since only one person can go."

"I wish they'd at least let two people in. It would be nice to go with a friend."

Clark laughed. "Yeah, well, it's been over a hundred years since they let anybody from the outborder in the college. They probably want to make sure we're not a bunch of barbarians out here before they go letting in two at a time." He sobered. "We're making history, Katie. Whoever is going."

"Why do you think they picked our village?" Katie asked.

"Blackwood's probably not the only village," Clark said. "They're probably picking a few graduates from other villages too. Just a handful of the best ones to see how we turned out."

Katie hugged Clark's waist, wishing that she had lied on her application. Allison had, creating a vivid picture of her desire to pursue a college education so she could return to her remote town and teach her fellow farmers the latest agricultural techniques for social development—even though everybody knew Allison was positioned to take over the school for Mrs. Nancy within the next two years.

Clark's essay read more truthfully, stating that he was already apprenticed as a doctor and wished to advance his skills as a surgeon, because the death of Dr. McConley had forced the entire village to treat wounds by reaching for their sewing kits and hoping for the best.

Katie had stated only the stark truth: her parents were dead, her sister wished to get married, her current livelihood was unsustainable, and she was desperate to experience the world beyond her neighbors. But selfishness didn't win scholarships.

Pangs of regret surged up her body, and she tightened her arms against Clark's waist. There was the other loss for her today; whether Clark or Allison won the coveted scholarship, one of them would be leaving tomorrow to live in one of the inborder cities. Even if it was Allison, without the excuse of school, she and Clark were going to have a hard time orbiting around each other. She was losing either one or both of her best friends.

"They're going to pick you, I know it," she whispered.

"I don't," Clark said. "They might pick you."

"They're not going to pick me," Katie replied.

"You don't know that."

"You and Allison are better students than me."

"Of course we are," Clark said. He turned his face to glance back at her, adding, "We have candles."

"I have candles!"

"Your candles are bacon grease spooned into an orange peel."

"It works...ish."

Clark huffed a short laugh. "Ish. I'm just saying I don't think you're really third in the class as far as brains go." He picked at the fraying leather. "Besides, we don't even know that they'll choose on school performance. Maybe they'll base it on family background. Your grandfather was from the inborder, wasn't he, before the Blackout? Maybe you could find some relatives still living there and see if they could get you in. I mean...if you don't want to stay with your sister."

"I do want to stay with my sister. It's her husband I'm not sure about."

"Why don't you like Jeremy?"

"His eyes are too small."

"He can't help that."

"Ears are too big."

"Can't help that either."

She sighed. "He didn't even finish third grade."

"Most of the villagers didn't finish school," Clark said. "He can read and write and add and subtract. He's running a good farm."

"It's a pig farm!"

"Yeah, it's a pig farm," Clark said. "Which means no matter how bad things get, Mallory won't have to go without food. And if it's meat, she's never going to starve."

Katie's eyes filled as the truth came out. "Yeah, but I don't want my sister to marry an ugly, uneducated man just so we don't starve." Her nose began to run, and she wiped it with her sleeve.

Clark rode a minute without saying anything before he asked, "You really think she doesn't want to marry him?"

"I don't know," Katie said.

"Because I know for a fact that Jeremy really wants to marry her. She's all he's talked about for the last three weeks."

Katie huffed a laugh.

"You think maybe you're really just upset because he's stealing your sister?" Clark asked gently.

"Maybe."

"That's how I felt when David moved out and got married. But we've all got to do it sooner or later."

"Do we?"

"Don't you want to?" Clark asked.

Her face heated, but she answered quickly, "Says the man with unlimited options."

Clark snorted. "Trust me, my options are extremely limited."

He turned to the left of the forked road, and the horse's ears flickered toward the girl who waited near the gate. The skirt of her gray dress flapped loosely as she used one foot to rub the back of the sock that peeked from her cracked shoes. Allison's face mirrored Katie's gloom as she sent a small smile. Strands of red hair escaped the braid she'd used to capture her wiry curls.

Clark swung down from his perch, handing the reins to Katie before he laced his fingers to offer Allison a step. But Allison ignored the gesture, instead peering up at Katie.

"I didn't sleep at all last night," she said. "Let's make a promise that no matter who gets the scholarship, we're all still going to be friends. We'll always be friends."

Katie blinked as logic broke up the sentimentality. "Whoever gets the scholarship won't even be here. I mean, we won't be enemies, but we're not exactly going to be talking."

"In our hearts," Allison amended. "Besides, I'm coming back—I mean, if I get it. You guys are too." Her eyes flickered down to Clark before she looked back up to Katie. "Aren't you?"

Katie shrugged. She scooted forward on the horse to make room for her friend. "I'm not getting it," she admitted, "so it doesn't matter. But I do want to go to the inborder someday, even if I have to find another way."

"Waiting," Clark interrupted, still frozen in his stoop.

Allison sighed, stuck her crusted boot into his hands and swung herself behind Katie. Katie waited until Clark had brushed the mud from his fingers before offering him the reins. He grabbed them and tugged the horse forward.

"They kill people who sneak past the inborder," Allison said quietly.

"I know." Katie felt the sob swell in her throat and held her breath again. Clark's lips pressed together. Allison let out a sigh. No one spoke again.

The schoolhouse stood at the edge of town, created by notched logs forming a square with six gaps for windows and a thatched roof. It had been constructed by hand, led by one man who protested the closing of the state-run institutions following the Blackout.

His wife had served as the first teacher, offering traditional hours that had shrunk with each generation until it leveled out, offering mornings of intensive study that released at noon so the young people could return to the tasks that ensured their community survived. One by one, most of Katie's older classmates had stopped attending at all, forced to stay in their family's fields or workshops. Even Allison's father had threatened to pull her, until she'd arranged to become the next teacher.

Katie's frowned dipped as she slid off the horse. After today, there would be nothing left here for her. She'd taken every lesson, had read every word in every book. The school may offer a plethora of nice memories, but there was nothing more it could teach her. She clutched the last of her books as she stepped toward the building.

But Clark grabbed her elbow, calling in a low tone, "Katie."

Allison's eyes darted toward them, then locked ahead on the school, and she marched out of earshot.

"If I get the scholarship," Clark said, "maybe I could find a way to bring you to the city too."

"How?"

"We could..." His eyes dropped. "I mean... I don't know, but I'll try."

Katie began a reply, but the wind blew a clump of hair into her mouth, carrying the smell of leather from the saddle shop across the street where Clark's uncle worked. She tucked her hair back into the braid. Clark glanced toward the shop as the man stepped into the doorway, making sure the two knew they were being watched.

Clark dropped her hand. He turned to grab his horse's reins and snapped them against the log fence, sending them spiraling into tight loops that allowed the animal only a modest graze.

Katie blinked, feeling hope spring like a seedling but squashed it like it was a cutworm. She avoided his eyes, turning toward the schoolroom as she said, "Clark...please don't make me promises you can't keep."

The Letter

KATIE ALMOST WISHED the man from the city had never announced the scholarship. As exciting as it was that a villager would see or do what had been denied for three generations, the anticipation had quickly turned to agony. The announcement, application process, and the monthlong wait for the result had infiltrated her ability to plan for her future or even chat normally with her friends. It was hard to enjoy their last school day when every second nudged them closer to the moment someone's life would change forever, and the others would have their fates sealed as citizens forever trapped in the outborder village of Blackwater.

Allison was right. They would have to make a concerted effort to remain friends. With every class, Katie compared her performance to Allison's quick answers with a growing dismay. She could only chew her lip and resolve not to resent either Clark or Allison, no matter how many years she was forced to spend earning her keep on a pig farm and dependent on the good will and income of her brother-in-law.

As noon crept closer, she became so nauseous she doubted she could eat anything. The school day ended before Tucker and his rusted delivery truck had returned from the borders of the city. No one walking back from the stores in town had seen hide or hair of him.

Katie stepped off the rotted wooden sidewalk and walked on the packed road instead, setting her mind on the next task: change into her new dress and meet Mallory in the town square for one final hug before she lost her sister to the arms of a man.

"Katie!" Clark jogged alongside his horse to catch up to her. But once he did, he didn't say anything, just kept opening his mouth, then catching each word before it actually left. She waited for him to gather his thoughts and was finally rewarded with a rushed, "If I can't get you to the inborder...if I even get there...will you wait for me?"

Katie stopped walking, so stunned she could only manage to blink.

"We could get married if we both decided to wait."

"Until you get back?" Katie asked.

He winced. "Maybe longer. We'd have to wait until my dad died."

"Your dad?" Katie sputtered. "That could be forty years from now."

"Probably more like ten or...maybe twenty but..." Clark tapered off. "But I'll wait if you will."

"Why couldn't we just get married?" Katie asked.

Clark stuck his hands into his pockets. "He said if I married you, he'd write me out of the will. But maybe we could win him over. Or if I went to the city, maybe I could get wealthy enough on my own."

The world reeled. Katie swayed with it. "I never liked you because of your wealth, Clark. But if it means that much to you, you should probably pick someone else."

His face slacked, then paled. "Katie, it's not that simple."

"Just enjoy your party tonight," she said. "We'll have at least two years to figure out our futures."

And fortunes.

She walked away, gripping her skirt to keep her fingers from trembling as her mind frantically sorted through the onslaught of emotions and thoughts, finally consolidating into an intense throb of regret.

She shoved the door to Katherine's seamstress shop harder than necessary. Neatly-folded squares of material made from the cotton of her own farm lined a long wooden table near the window. Old tin cans held salvaged buttons, rolled zippers, and a few old rhinestones that had been pulled off tattered clothes before they were turned into rags.

Katherine was kneeling in front of Ms. Bonnie Blackwell, pinning material just above the stout woman's ankles. The seamstress sent Katie a quick smile that lifted only the corners of her mouth because the rest of her lips were pinching straight pins.

"Katie!" Bonnie called before Katie could hide behind a shelf. "Did Tucker bring the letter yet?"

"Not yet," Katie said.

Bonnie moved to the counter, pulling her hem from Katherine's fingers and leaving the young woman to jab the air. "I have a gift for your sister. Please be sure and give it to her with my good wishes. I don't expect I'll be able to attend the wedding myself, but I want her to know that I am in no way disapproving of her marriage. I'm very happy for her. She couldn't do better than Jeremy."

The box was round, likely containing one of Bonnie's creations, for the woman passed her ample free time by elaborately decorating hats to protect the local girls from the blazing sun.

"I will give it to her, thank you," Katie said.

"I'll make one for you too," Bonnie promised. "When you get married. I happen to know that someone has been waiting for you to finish school. Now that your time will be freed up for homemaking, I wouldn't be shocked if he finally got around to speaking up."

Katie recoiled slightly, eyeing the woman, wondering if she was approving or fishing. "And who would that be?"

"Have you ever noticed the way that Sam watches you?"

"Sam?"

The woman nodded. "He would be a good match for you. I know he's terribly shy, but I'm sure once you grew comfortable with each other, he would open up and talk more."

"Sam's never said more than three words to me."

The woman's head tipped, almost sympathetically. "Perhaps he would if you stopped standing so close to Clark."

Katherine stood, smoothing the wrinkles out of her own dress. "I'm finished with the pinning, Ms. Blackwell. You can change out of the gown now."

"Well, that was quick and painless, wasn't it?" Ms. Blackwell flashed them both a jovial smile and moved to the back room.

Katie closed her eyes, then forced them open to raise her eyebrows toward Katherine. "Thank you."

Katherine grimaced as she stepped close. "Don't thank me yet. I'm awfully sorry. I stayed up until my candle burned out but...I don't have your dress finished."

"The wedding is in an hour," Katie sputtered.

"I know. I've worked every evening later than I normally do, but Georgia Blackwell needed to let out her dress, and Karina ordered an entirely new one. There's some sort of Blackwell party going on tonight."

"Well, I guess it's good for business," Katie managed.

Katherine shook her head in an apology, "I'm really sorry, Katie. I know I had your order first, but you know how it is. I have your bodice finished, but I'm not done with the lining and the skirt is basted on, but I didn't get time to attach it properly and the hem's not finished. I can finish it tonight though, I swear, and you can at least have it tomorrow...if you win the scholarship."

"I doubt I'll win," Katie said. "It's all right, though. It's Mallory's wedding anyway. I'll just wear this, and you can finish the dress this week after you get some sleep."

She eyed her friend hard.

Katherine smiled, whispering, "Thank you."

Katie dropped her voice to a mimicking whisper. "Now, I'm going to run before Ms. Blackwell comes back."

Katherine widened her eyes in agreement and mouthed, "Sam?"

Both girls wrinkled their noses at the mere idea.

Katie hurried from the shop, keenly aware of every faint stain in her dress. It took three swallows to banish her disappointment. She rounded the corner faster than usual, smacking straight into a man.

She managed to stop with her nose nearly against the thick gray material of a suit, but when she lifted her head, she was greeted with a familiar set of large ears. She recognized the brown hair, squinty eyes, and crooked smile, but she still gaped. "Jeremy! I almost didn't recognize you without your beard."

Jeremy's dimples sunk his cheeks as he offered a grimace. "Yeah. I thought I'd clean myself up for Mallory, so I got my hair cut and..." He swallowed so hard she saw the bob of his Adam's apple. "I didn't do myself any favors, did I?"

He certainly had not.

Without the beard, Jeremy's hair was neatly trimmed and looked well-kept, but the shorter length only accentuated his ears and highlighted his protruding brows. The collar of his dress shirt had chaffed a red line into his neck. He was sweating profusely.

For the first time in her life, she couldn't rouse a shred of dislike for the man.

"Well," she stammered, then forced the strain from her voice. "It's not that bad. It's probably just that we're not used to seeing you without a beard. And I know for a fact that Mallory always preferred the boys without the beards."

The last line worked, and the wrinkles smoothed out of his forehead. His shoulders relaxed. His mouth perked slightly, and she swore even his ears lifted. "I thought she did," he said, sticking his hands into his pockets. "I remembered that. I was on my way to the square. Do you want to walk with me?"

"Sure," Katie replied and resigned herself to his company.

"Did you hear about the scholarship yet?"

"Nope," she answered.

"I didn't think so," he said. "I've been watching for Tucker's truck all day, but I hadn't seen it. I hope they pick you. You're a smart girl. Can you imagine one of us just going out there? I don't have hard feelings toward the Blackwells, but I'd love to see their faces if somebody else got picked for once."

He grinned, and she felt the smallest smile rise. Revenge on the Blackwells would taste sweeter if her best friend wasn't one of them. She almost asked Jeremy if he could imagine the Blackwells' faces if one of them picked her for a wife, but she pressed her lips together. Clark had picked her and that made her heart warm, but he'd also chosen his inherited wealth over her and that made the feeling burn away. She wasn't sure if she was flattered, sentimental, or angry. Nor was she sure that Jeremy's generosity would accommodate a ten-year secret engagement.

"Ms. Blackwell sent Mallory a hat," she said instead and lifted the box. "Hope you're prepared for frills and dried flowers."

Jeremy took the box from her without asking if she'd like him to carry it. His eyes sparkled. "Oh, I don't mind if Mallory likes it. There's not many things in my house nice to look at, but I guess lots of frills may be coming in after you ladies get at it."

Katie laughed. "We've already packed the curtains."

She should thank him. It was the perfect moment to acknowledge that she was aware of the sacrifice he and Mallory were making, giving up their short time to enjoy each other's company without anyone else in the house before kids were added to the mix. But she couldn't. It was too awkward. And part of her felt it was unnecessary. After all, she wouldn't be impeding on Jeremy's life if he hadn't first inserted himself into hers.

But he saw Mallory all the way from across the square, and the woman turned like she'd sensed his arrival. The two smiled at each other and Katie finally accepted that there was no way either of them were going to change their mind.

In her grandfather's day, the square had held a stately brick building where men had once been defended whether they were guilty or innocent. After the Blackout, it had been used to house travelers who were trying to find their way home. And then the foreign army had come, killing citizens, raiding houses, and taking up residence in the courthouse.

They might still be there, except Cameron Blackwell had rallied the entire village, claiming that it was better to die courageously than to live enslaved, and they'd resolved the situation by rounding up anyone they didn't recognize, locking them into the building, and burning it down without any trial by jury.

They'd expected a retaliation, but no second group of soldiers had ever come, even though Katie's father had spent his youth patrolling the borders of Blackwell. By the time he'd gotten married, the government had regained control and begun a program to rebuild the cities, leaving the remote territories largely on their own. As long as they paid their taxes and offered a steady supply of goods for trade, nobody bothered much with Blackwood, leaving the village in relative peace.

The bricks of the courthouse had been repurposed to add fireplaces to the houses as winters cycled and no electricity was restored. The live oak trees had been allowed to grow over the old sidewalks, framing the open space and leaving only the building's foundation to host happier events like dances and weddings.

Katie kept busy, helping the older guests unload their chairs as their wagons arrived. Even the Blackwells began to show up, since Tucker still hadn't brought the letter that would usher in Clark's party. Clark didn't come himself until five minutes before the ceremony started and kept to the opposite side of the crowd.

Katie stood, glad most eyes were on the couple who were greeting the preacher near the table that held both the rings and the cake. She backed up a little, hoping to be lost in the crowd.

Allison stepped beside her. Her friend took both of her hands, tilting her head. "You look so sad."

The comment almost broke her, and Katie pulled her friend in for a hug, swallowing before she asked, "Will you stay with me at my house tonight?"

"Sure," Allison replied, then pulled back. "What happened to your new dress?"

Katie huffed a laugh because no one else had even noticed. "The Blackwells."

"No!" Allison offered the appropriate gasp, then glanced down at her own attire. "Do you want to wear mine?"

"No, it's okay," Katie said. "Trust me, the dress is the least of the drama."

"Oh you must share," Allison said, but the ceremony began before Katie could.

Jeremy's grin lifted his ears. The appendages seemed to have a life of their own and regularly rose and fell as he captured Mallory with promises of provision. His suit—which looked suspiciously like one of Clark's—hung stiffly, shifting as he pulled first at the collar, then at the sleeves where the white undershirt peeked from beneath his coat.

Mallory, on the other hand, had transformed from a quiet woman with a somber expression into a girl that could have captured even a Blackwell's attention had she not just signed her availability away. Her light brown hair wrapped her head in a crown braid that secured sprigs of goldenrod. Katherine had altered the wedding dress, yet again, to fit Mallory's slim waist with no need for a colorful back to expand the bodice as Lori had used when she'd worn the dress last month or a second skirt layered beneath to extend the hem as Jane had improvised for her wedding. Katie wondered if the libraries in the inborder offered more than one choice of wedding gown, but it was nice to see Mallory in a gown that had enough material to reach her ankles.

Katie swallowed, doubting the dress could ever be hemmed and darted enough to fit her own tiny frame. She'd stopped growing when she was fourteen, her height settling a full inch under five feet, and she could see the outline of her ribs even without sucking in her stomach. She had managed a few slight curves that showed she was not actually a child, but she was far from curvaceous.

As Jeremy slipped his grandmother's ring onto Mallory's finger, the clouds broke apart like they had been waiting for that very moment. Katie's stomach flipped again but looking at Mallory's face helped, because she was beginning to feel like maybe—for whatever reason—Mallory really did want to marry

Jeremy. Katie caught a tiny flicker of happiness and fanned the feeling for all it was worth. She even managed to cheer with Allison when the couple kissed.

The cake was cut and devoured. The opening stanza of a violin ushered in the first dance between husband and wife. Everyone else began their customary creeping: young boys crept back to the cake table to pick up any stray crumbs, older boys edged closer to the girls they were thinking about asking for the next dance, and a few adults sneaked away toward home.

Katie glanced toward Clark, but he had planted himself in the shadows of the cedar tree, studying his wine glass and successfully avoiding every inviting eye, though there were plenty of them.

Dancing with a Blackwell man transformed you, according to your rank, into either a starlet or a slut. Katie knew this because she'd danced with Clark two years ago, just once. She'd gone to sleep with stars in her eyes and had woken to a year of canceled invitations, stony silences on one side, and whispered accusations of gold-digging on the other.

Only Allison had remained loyal, ready to shove her toward Clark or drag her away at Katie's command. Most often it had been away, for though Clark lived on the family fringe, at the end of the day he was still a Blackwell.

"Even if he doesn't ask you," Allison's voice floated into her ear, "he's thinking about it."

"He won't ask," Katie said. "It's all right. I'd rather he didn't."

Allison threw her a skeptical glance.

"I would!" she defended. "School is over. It's...everything's over."

"You don't know that."

Over the rapid notes of Gabe's violin, a distant drone transformed into a rattling engine. Tucker's truck rolled onto the grass, stopping inches from the sawhorses and sheets of wood that had been lined up as tables.

"It will be," Katie answered.

Allison froze, then turned almost a pitying glance toward her. "We'll still be friends, no matter what."

The crowd flowed toward the truck, each mind suddenly turned toward treasure from the inborder: glass jars, paint, duct tape. Especially duct tape.

"Now y'all stand back!" Mr. Tucker flapped his arms like he was surrounded by chickens as he clambered out of the cab. "Everybody will get their stuff before you go home, don't worry. You don't want to be holding it all night, do ya?"

He spoke fast, his pitch increasing with his pace, and he clutched three envelopes. Katie froze. She cast a worried look toward the bride, but Mallory only lifted her eyebrows, feigning the excited belief that Katie was still in the running.

Jeremy's ears bounced as he called out, "'Fess up, Tucker! Did you peek?"

Tucker stopped, drew his hand to press the envelopes against his chest and declared, "Tucker does not peek!"

He spoke the truth, for the envelopes he delivered to Allison and Katie were still sealed, but he winked toward Katie even as he spoke to both. "Good luck, girls."

Allison clutched her envelope, managing a flickering smile. Katie suddenly wished she had danced with Clark because he had paled so much it looked like someone might need to catch him if he passed out. But he recovered with a breath, took his own envelope as he thanked Tucker, and bore the attention of the majority of spectators. His fingers trembled as he broke the seal, face whitening as his eyes dropped to the bottom of the letter. His expression remained neutral, but he swallowed and shut the paper, announcing in a tone so steady it took people a moment to register his words. "I didn't get in."

Allison stared, then clawed open her envelope. Katie slipped her fingers beneath her own seal and pulled the folded paper out, noting with excitement that one side was completely blank with ample room for writing.

"I didn't either," Allison's voice broke as she spoke up.

Katie glanced to the crestfallen face next to her. For a whole month the unspoken question of who would go had hung over the group. It had never occurred to any of that none of them would go.

Until now.

Allison's eyes met Katie's, matching her panic, and they turned simultaneously toward Katie's letter.

Congratulations.

Katie saw only the first word before Allison grabbed her arm. "Katie, you got it!" Allison's squeal buzzed her ear. "Katie got it! Katie's going!"

Katie's mouth fell, the only part of her body that could move until her friend crushed her in a hug.

"Congratulations, Katie." Allison's excitement drained into a whisper.

Katie held her friend, feeling the girl's arms tremble. Every eye was on her. She shrank beneath the force of the stares, glancing to the kindest of the faces. Several people cheered. A few Blackwells blinked, unsure how to react to the rejection of one of their own, though Clark's father's face reflected only a growing relief.

Tucker clapped so hard that dust rose from his oversized gloves. Mallory covered her mouth but smiled behind it. Her new husband grinned outright. Clark's face remained masked, but he managed to nod with approval when Katie's eyes met his. Allison pulled back, managed one last smile, then burst into tears.

Crossing the Border

DESPITE HER PROMISE of nothing changing, Allison hadn't spent the night or even shown up in the morning to say goodbye. Katherine had, finally bringing the finished dress, glowing with the idea that it would be seen by city people. The material was a creamy yellow, dyed with the goldenrod that grew nearly everywhere. It was plain but cheerful. Katie suspected, by the dark circles under her friend's eyes, that Katherine had stayed up all night working on it.

"I'm glad it was you, Katie," Katherine said. "You've always worked so hard. What are you going to study?"

"I don't even know," Katie sputtered. "I refused to think about it. I didn't think I'd get in."

"Well, I know you'll do a great job, whatever you decide," Katherine said. "Please write and tell us about it."

"Won't that seem like bragging?"

"Not if it's true. Besides, we all need something to daydream about. The rest of our futures are set." Katherine's smile wavered before she forced it back. She squeezed Katie in a tight hug, then rushed out the door, already running late.

Katie packed her things in a crate, contemplating taking the quilt, but she decided to leave it for Mallory. Even in Texas, the winters were miserably cold. She took only her clothing, wondering how different her life would be when she returned.

The screen door creaked and slammed, its sound suddenly nostalgic. It wasn't likely her house would survive, for Mr. Blackwell was the first to throw down money for any scrap of land that came up for sale and once he bought it, he'd dismantle everything to be sold for repurposing. Their land was prime for farming and his workers already had homes. It made her sick and also glad her father couldn't see his farm being taken over by the man he most despised.

Because once upon a time, a young Alexander Hunter had made the mistake of laughing at a young Graham Blackwell's attempt to spell the word 'narcissistic.' Graham had retaliated by gathering all his cousins to jump Alex while he was out picking cotton, leaving the bloodied boy slumped over his sack.

Then Alex had swooped in and stolen the most beautiful girl in town before Graham had worked up the courage to walk over and ask her out. Graham had countered the move by convincing his father to recruit Alex to patrol the borders during school hours, so he didn't have any chance to see Madeline anymore. So Madeline had responded by publicly accompanying one man by day and secretly courting a different man by night.

And then Mallory had come along and brought an uneasy ending to the dispute. Katie thought of that often: what her world might have been if Clark didn't exist, and she was Mr. Blackwell's daughter instead of the product of his lost battle. As it was, it was Clark who lived with his father's anger and a mother who knew she was the second choice.

She sighed. Maybe she was being unfair to Clark, to expect him to further humiliate Mayor Blackwell by publicly declaring that he had fallen in love with Madeline's daughter.

It was strange to reach the town and find everyone going about their business. A few villagers smiled at her. Several called out or offered a quick hug. But it was a normal day for them, another race to bring in crops, to load their offerings onto Tucker's truck, to begin their apprenticeships on time. Even Clark looked harried and pale, clutching his satchel as he rode down the street.

She swallowed, uncertain if she should call out or leave him alone. Hating that their last interaction was an argument about futures, that now she wasn't even sure what he was thinking. But he spotted her and turned his horse to cross the street. He slid off the animal, his face stoic with the famous Blackwell mask.

"I'm sorry about yesterday," he said.

Katie swallowed. "Me too."

The silence stretched as she tried to think of a way to ask if he still hoped she would wait or if his first rejection had shaken him into reality.

"Maybe I can find a way to get you there," she teased weakly.

He smiled with no mirth. "I think I may have been unrealistic in that regard. Even my father's money can't get me into the inborder." He took a breath. "But I also realized last night that a half-trained doctor is better than no doctor. So I guess I'd better stay here."

"I guess you'd better," she echoed.

He struggled for a sentence, then shrugged and said, "Have fun."

He opened his satchel and dug out a package wrapped in butcher paper, shoving it into her hands. Then he snapped his hat back onto his head in his usual manner and mounted his horse, now properly saddled with no room for her. He didn't look back.

And neither could she.

She clutched the envelope and the package, feeling her throat tighten as she searched for Tucker's truck but—as usual—he was running late. So late that there was no escaping Mayor Blackwell.

He offered her a smile that looked like Clark's but lacked its warmth. "I hope you realize the enormous opportunity you've been given," the man said.

"I do," she answered, a tad defiantly.

"My son and Allison will be held back for the rest of their lives after losing this chance," he said. "Our entire town will be judged on your performance and your attitude."

He eyed her. She tried to meet his stare but only managed to lift her eyes as far as his stiff collar.

"I have wanted to cross the border for my entire life," she said. "I am not going to squander this."

"See that you don't," he said. "And while you're there, find a way to stay there. You'll do far more for this village by continuing to represent our people in the inborder than you would by returning here. Jeremy will have enough mouths to feed, and Clark will be married before you return. You'd do better to make yourself a life in the inborder. Understood?"

"Understood," she answered. She lifted her chin. "Not to be mistaken with agreed. You don't own me, Mr. Blackwell."

He almost smiled, but his face masked again. "No," he said. "I do not own you. But I do own the well your sister and her husband drink from. And we all know what happens if you try to live off the river water."

Her heart burned as panic was swamped by rage. She almost replied that he wouldn't dare, but the problem was that he would. So she stood shaking, trying to hold back any words she would regret and resolving that not only would she come back, but she would come back in a far more powerful position than she was in now.

"Katie!" Tucker's voice broke the tension.

He ignored the mayor's smirk as he reached for her crate, putting his body between them. He grinned. "Ready for a new life?"

"Yes," she said, and escaped the man who ran her town.

She didn't successfully hide her tears, but Tucker must have figured they were from so many goodbyes. She stared out of the window of the truck as the tires kicked up dust and the wind whistled through the windows, lashing her hair into her eyes. She tucked the flying strands behind her ear, irritated that her hair was too slick and thin to stay where she wanted it.

"You're gonna love the city, Katie," Tucker said. "There are things there you never even imagined. When you finish up in four years, you gotta at least come back for a visit and tell poor Tucker all about it. I seen those buildings in the distance all my life, but I never been up close."

"Not ever?"

"I'm only allowed to go to the border," Tucker said. "Traders from the inborder come out. I give 'em what they need and get what we need. But my truck ain't cleared to go in." He eyed Katie. "You gotta stick close to me at the market. Some of those merchants will sell anything they can get their hands on—including women. You'll be safe in the city with your sponsor family. But you got to be careful on the border."

Katie gulped for air, imagining a world where every face belonged to a stranger.

Tucker nudged her with his elbow. "Now I come here every first Saturday. I know you'll be busy with school and all that, and maybe you can't get over to the market. But if you can, have somebody bring a letter to my truck, and that way we'll all know how you're doing."

Katie swallowed, suddenly envisioning every word she wrote being read at the village church service. Anything bad would make Mallory worry. Anything good would make Allison cry.

"I'll try," she said.

She turned her eyes away before he could see her tears pool again. They blurred the limbs of the live oaks that swept in gnarled loops only inches off the ground. Brushwood and mesquite trees grew between them, creating a thick maze of foliage.

The tires spat the last of the rocks behind them as they hit paved asphalt. Katie worked a foot beneath her to see better out of the windshield as a dark, smooth road stretched ahead like a wide ribbon. The truck quieted, even though the wind still blew through the windows. Sunlight glinted off the river, glimmering between the trees before it wound away from them again. That was one comfort. The river, at least, would go with her, or rather leave her, for it flowed from the city to the village.

"Too bad the river flows downstream and not up," she said. "Y'all could just drop a note in a bottle."

"You got a better chance of somebody finding a note you send to us, than one coming to you. You're gonna be too busy to fish, and them town people don't wash their clothes in the river."

She blinked. "They don't wash their clothes?"

"They do, just not in the river. They got machines to wash for them. And they don't have to crank them to make them run, neither."

"How do they run?"

"With electricity. They got electricity there, just like our folks did before the Blackout."

"Huh." She picked at the twine that held the wrapping around her package. "I don't know if Dad would want me go anywhere near electricity."

"He'd be a fool not to. Somebody's gotta get out of our village." He turned off the road onto a large field where people had set up tables and opened the back of trucks. "Did you remember to wash behind your ears?"

"Funny," Katie threw back, and her driver just grinned.

The two sponsors stood out in the sea of vendors, dressed like they'd intended to show up for Mallory's wedding rather than picking up a new student at a market. The man stood with his hands in the pockets of a traditional suit, gray with silver stripes running down the pattern. He wore a dark silver tie accentuated with lines, only now they ran at a slant. Even his hair seemed in on the act, dark in the middle, but framed with silver that grew near his temples and highlighted the path over his ears. He peered at Katie and his mouth turned downward, Blackwell-style. Katie felt a twinge of fear as she stepped onto grass that had been crushed by a dozen tires.

But the woman glowed. Her hair was the same blonde as Katie's, but it was cut short and curled against her head. Her blue eyes were framed with darkened lashes. She wore a tailored bodice of pale peach, matching a pleated skirt that rippled softly with each movement. Her shoes were mostly straps wrapping her feet and ankles, the heel only a peg. She was even more elegant than Mrs. Blackwell.

"Katie!" the woman called.

Katie instinctively pulled her shoulders back with movements she'd practiced in front of the mirror since she was six. She watched, enchanted as the lady approached with a smile that never wavered. Her arms expanded, wrapping around Katie like it was a reunion instead of a meeting. She smelled like chamomile.

Senses overwhelmed, Katie choked again, for something in the hug was genuine and made her miss her mother. And just as suddenly, she was pushed away. The woman studied her, saying, "We are so glad to have you. Aren't we, Richard?"

The man tore his eyes from inspecting the dent in Tucker's truck. "Hmm? Oh. Yes."

"I am Mrs. Alcott. This is my husband, Richard. You may call him Mr. Alcott. We've set up a room all to yourself at our home. You're going to just love it." Mrs. Alcott tugged gently on Katie's hand, guiding her toward a distant line of cars. "All the things in the room are new. We bought them just for you, though I had to guess the size for the clothes. If they don't fit, we can always exchange them."

Katie glanced back, suddenly realizing she hadn't said goodbye to Tucker, but he was already twenty feet behind them. She turned back to Mrs. Alcott, but before she could ask to run back, the woman asked her own question.

"Have you ever slept on FreeFibre sheets? No? Oh, you will love them! We just got a set for ourselves, and they are the softest things you can imagine. Just like butter!"

Sleeping in butter sounded slimy. Katie blinked, half turned back to the men, but they were breaking apart.

Mr. Tucker waved. Then he put his hand to his mouth and shouted, "Don't forget, the first Saturday!"

Katie waved back and, as her arm fell, Mrs. Alcott swept it against her side, cradling her as they walked.

"You're very thin," the woman said. "You must be hungry. Richard tells me people from the woods are always hungry. But just hang on a little bit longer. We have a treat for you tonight. We're having lobster. I don't suppose you've ever had it. It grows in the water, Richard says. Did you know there are places in the world where there's nothing except water for as far as you can see? Some days when the sky and water are all blue or all gray, you can't even tell one from the other. It's just one big block of nothingness. I've seen it. Richard and I travel a lot."

The woman's words piled in Katie's head, creating disjointed pictures, but Mr. Alcott did nothing to aid when he caught up, carrying the crate with Katie's clothing. As the trio passed through the line of tables, items were thrust at them from every side. Some traders fell into step behind them, clamoring until Mr. Alcott shouted them away. "No, no, we're not here to buy today."

Katie hugged Clark's gift against her chest, shielding herself from the throng.

"Want me to hold your package?" Mrs. Alcott asked.

"No, thanks. I'll keep it with me."

"What is it?"

"I don't know." She honestly wasn't sure she wanted to know. It was like having a piece of Clark with her, but not Clark himself. Enough to bind her to him, but not enough to have him. She sighed. "Clark gave it to me just before I left."

"Clark?" The woman smiled and elbowed her. "Is that a boyfriend?"

Katie winced. "We're just friends."

"I see," the woman said.

A few persistent hopefuls followed them down the row of vehicles until they reached a black, smoothly curved car.

Mr. Alcott opened the door and shoved the crate across the seat. He grabbed Katie's arm to hurry her in and nearly slammed the door on her foot. Mrs. Alcott slid into her seat, and he locked the doors while he rounded the hood.

A merchant yanked on Katie's door, holding a pendent to swing in her view. "I have a lovely necklace for you, sweetheart!"

27

She stared through the tinted window, wondering if this was how Clark felt every day.

"Leave us alone!" Mr. Alcott roared.

The man stepped back with a surprised glance as Mr. Alcott unlocked the driver's door by key and slid inside. He let out a harsh breath and glared at his wife. "I told you it was a bad idea to pick her up here."

"Where else could we have picked her up?" Mrs. Alcott asked.

"Her village."

"Then we would have had three times this rabble! Besides, last time I went there, the water made me sick, remember?"

Katie shifted to try to see more of the woman's face. "You've been to Blackwood?"

"Only once while we were traveling a few months ago," Mrs. Alcott said. "We saw you. From a distance."

Mr. Alcott started the car and revved the engine. He inched the vehicle forward and the crowd scattered like oil away from a drop of water, but Katie didn't start to breathe easier until they had left the market behind. About a mile down the road, the car stopped again.

Mrs. Alcott turned in her seat, her voice dropping into a confiding tone. "We do have one little problem, Katie. You're not vaccinated, and they won't let you into the city until you are. Now, we can get it done, but not today. So—just for today—you're going to have to hide in the car. Once we get you across safely, you can stay at our house, and we'll take you tomorrow to get everything all set up for school."

Katie hugged Clark's gift closer to her chest, eyeing the floorboard with trepidation. "Isn't that illegal?"

"It's not a big deal, really. The medical center is closed today, but we couldn't come tomorrow," Mrs. Alcott said. "We won't be taking you to any of the stores, just straight to our home, so it really isn't a problem. They just don't need to know there are three people in the car, instead of two, when we go through the checkpoint. We'll put you on the floorboard and cover you with the packages, and we'll be good to go."

Katie's heart sped. She glanced behind down the deserted road. She swallowed, remembering Tucker's warning about the merchants catching her alone. "Well, I guess that would be all right."

Already two seats were filled with colorful shopping bags, and the floorboard allowed only a small gap. Katie crawled into it and pulled her legs to her chest. The bags Mrs. Alcott covered her with felt like they were each filled with only one light thing.

Good thing they'd chosen her for the scholarship. There was no way that Clark could have fit into this spot. Katie waited until the door in front had shut again and the car began to jostle its way over the uneven ground before she asked, "What does vaccinated mean?"

"Inoculated," Mr. Alcott answered. "So, you don't get sick while you're here or spread any village sicknesses to us."

"Like the sickness in the river water?" she asked.

"Oh, it can be in the water, in air, anywhere," Mrs. Alcott said. "Sometimes it just doesn't work well when village and city people mix. But they told us you were healthy, and you appear to be so, so we should have nothing to worry about."

"Who told you I was healthy?" Katie asked.

"The scholarship people."

"How could they know?"

"I suppose they asked your local doctor."

Katie frowned. "Our local doctor died. Clark is the doctor now. Nobody asked him. He would have told me...I think."

Katie shifted, trying to relieve the shoulder she was lying on, wondering what inoculated meant. She may find lots of words here she didn't know. She didn't know there was anything in the world that could keep one from getting sick. What could such a thing do for her town?

She could bring an inoculator—or whatever it was—to Clark. He could be the most successful doctor they'd ever had. Perhaps then his family would accept her. Perhaps she could return to the village dressing and walking as elegantly as Mrs. Alcott. Even Mr. Blackwell couldn't stop her from such a transformation.

The Shift

WHEN MR. ALCOTT FINALLY opened the door, Katie saw grass first, clipped short and even, like someone had taken a scythe to the entire lawn in one straight motion. Then a stately red brick house so tall she had to lift her chin to see the gray roof with neat rows of tiles. A concrete slab wound its way to a white door with no screen. There were no windows, even though every other house on the street had them.

Katie stopped. "Where are your windows?"

"We don't need windows," Mrs. Alcott answered. "There are lights inside, so we can see perfectly fine. Houses are much safer without them. Our home is newer than those other ones. It was built just for us when the government hired Richard. Some of the neighbors aren't very nice."

Mr. Alcott cocked his head toward his wife, but replied evenly, "But you will be safe inside."

Katie swayed, glancing up and down the road, but she couldn't see anyone outside at all, so she followed the couple to the porch. Mr. Alcott removed a black rectangle from his pocket and pushed a series of buttons. The door slowly opened on its own, revealing an entryway where a glass table lined the wall. The white marble tile had been polished so much that it reflected her boots as it led into a larger room with carpet that blanketed the floor like fresh snow. Ivory walls rose, meeting tin ceiling titles. Two crystal chandeliers hung suspended above the room. Their bulbs were shaped like flames, but the light gave a steady glow from within their glass enclosures.

Katie inched forward, peering in every direction. The Alcotts relaxed, ignoring the room's luxury as they strode inside. Mr. Alcott set down the crate and shrugged off his coat, hanging it on a hook before he reached for his wife's blazer. The air was warm, though Katie couldn't see a fireplace.

She walked past the couple, entranced with the light. She nearly ran into the back of a couch that blocked the entryway and created a division between the rooms. She stopped, focusing on the main room, a sitting area with a second couch that faced her where a young man stared at her. He stood quickly, setting down a black container of food onto the short table in front of the couch.

She had never seen any face so uniform; his cheekbones were perfectly paralleled, his eyes the exact golden-brown color as his eyebrows and trimmed hair. His skin was smoother than she knew a guy's could be, as though someone had sanded the stubble right off his face.

Mr. Alcott was taller than any man she'd ever seen, but he was thin like he'd been stretched. This younger man was almost as tall, but also wide, like someone had tapped him with a wand and grown him in perfect proportions.

"Here we are, Neil," Mrs. Alcott said.

Neil stared, blinking rapidly. His lips parted, but he said nothing. He took a breath, then lost it at once.

"Well, aren't you going to say hello?" Mrs. Alcott prompted.

His fingers closed into a loose fist at his side, then relaxed again. He swallowed, took a deep breath, then spoke in a smooth tone that resonated deeper than Katie had expected. "Hello."

"Hi, I'm Katie," she said.

His eyes flickered to his father, glistening with panic like Clark's did whenever he was asked a question at school he didn't know.

"Hi?" he answered though it sounded more like a question.

"This is our son, Neil," Mrs. Alcott said.

Neil wet his lip, panted another breath, began to form a word, then shook his head. Blinked and swallowed.

"You'll have to forgive Neil," Mrs. Alcott said. "There's nothing wrong with his brain. The problem is in his vocal cords. It's difficult for him to speak. Other than that, he's completely normal. Neil, do you want to show Katie her room?"

Neil's eyes slit, fanning trails of fine lines like tiny cracks as he turned toward his father. Mr. Alcott held out Katie's crate. Neil's lips pinched, but he yanked the crate from the man and turned to stalk into a hallway. Katie fell into step behind him, staring at the white carpet that sank beneath her shoes.

The bedroom held a solid block of purple fabric from the blanket that had been tucked beneath the mattress. Two tiny white tables stood on opposite sides of the bed, with matching silver lamps that curved up, then over like they were trying to peer at the sleeper. Even the headboard created an S shape, sloping over the pillows.

Neil swung the crate onto a clear desk that almost blended in with the wall. He glanced into the top corner of the ceiling at a black half-circle, then turned to Katie. He was so tall that her eyes were level with his chest, close enough to see the buttons on his shirt move with his labored breath.

"Are you all right?" Katie asked.

Neil's breathing only grew harder. He glanced at the door, then her. He swallowed twice. His eyes slit again, before he growled and spun away from her, striding back out the door.

Katie stood frozen, hugging Clark's gift like it was Clark himself. She forced herself to move, to lay the package onto the desk. Her mind raced, working to make sense of what had just happened.

She was going to have to live with this guy? Why was he mad? Jealous? Had he tried for a scholarship and failed? Was he like the Blackwells and resenting sharing his space with someone so poor? Had she done something wrong?

She couldn't have. All she had said was hi. Maybe he didn't know what "hi" meant, maybe he thought it was something bad. But what kind of person wouldn't know how to say hi?

Mrs. Alcott stepped into the door with a bright smile. "I'm sure it all feels overwhelming at first, but you'll catch on," the woman said. "See the lights?" She continued without waiting for Katie to reply. "If you clap twice, they'll go out." She demonstrated, plunging Katie into deep darkness in the windowless room. "If you need to get up in the night, clap three times and..."

Light spilled from the lamps near the bed, bathing the woman in a dim red light. Her nose created a shadow between her eyes that distorted her features as she explained, "The red won't interfere with your melatonin levels, so you'll sleep better. If you clap once..." The main light returned to its normal color.

"How are you doing that?" Katie asked.

"Electricity," the woman explained. "Everything here is run by electricity. But it is limited, so be sure you turn out the lights when you're not using a room. If you use too many things at once, we'll go above our quota and the meter will cut it off. Neil hates the dark, and there's no way to turn them back on without calling someone to come fix it. And then we'll be fined. Richard hates fines. So only run a few things at a time. Got it?"

"I think so," Katie said.

The woman spun on her heels and led her to the room at the end of the hall.

"This is the bathroom," Mrs. Alcott said, ushering Katie to the door on the left. "This is where you will get ready in the mornings." She stepped to the counter with a ceramic sink, similar to what Katie used at home to wash her clothing before she drained the water into the garden. Only Mrs. Alcott swung her hand under the spout and water began to pour into the sink. It only lasted until the woman withdrew her hand. "You use this for washing your hands. That over there is the toilet. It's like an outhouse. You have those, don't you?"

"We have toilets," Katie said. "They're from before the Blackout. They just don't work anymore."

"Well, they work here," the woman said. "They're automatic too, so you don't even have to flush. Do you know how to work a shower?"

"A...shower?" Katie asked. "Like rain?"

Mrs. Alcott cocked her head, then let out a little laugh. "Well, I guess it is like rain."

Katie peeked down the hallway, glimpsing the men. Mr. Alcott stood with his body angled near Neil, his mouth moving in a steady flow of words. Neil rubbed his eye, listening and nodding.

Mrs. Alcott shut the door and smiled brightly at her. "This is a private room," she said, touching her finger to the round fixture on the door. It responded with a noise like a bolt sliding into a lock. "Just hold your finger here and the door locks, so no one will accidentally walk in on you."

Katie copied her action and the door unlocked. She pushed it open.

Mrs. Alcott's eyes met Katie's. "It's private. So, you must never be in here with anyone else. That is one of our rules."

Katie shifted, feeling embarrassment and anger rise in her chest. "We don't bathe in front of people at home either."

"Good." The woman smiled, reaching for a hairbrush. "Now, sit there." She motioned to a chair so clear that it blended in with the counter it sat beneath. "We have to get you ready for college. So, you can try the shower in a few moments. You'll love it. Just step under it, and it will come on like the sink. But we have to fix your hair first."

Katie blinked but obeyed, wondering why they should braid her hair before washing it. But the woman only loosened her braid, gently guiding the brush through her hair and stroking it with her free hand.

"I always wanted a daughter," she said. "You have beautiful hair. It's a pity it's so thin and long. Next time I go to the store, I'll get you some conditioner. My hairdresser has some that is wonderful."

She snapped her finger near a drawer. It made a whirring sound and opened slowly, revealing a display of combs, brushes, curlers, and a pair of steel scissors. She reached for the scissors.

Katie stood and backed against the wall. "What are you doing?"

"Well, you can't go to school looking like an outborder girl," the woman explained.

"I *am* an outborder girl."

"Trust me, darling. You don't want to let your peers know your background, scholarship or not. No one wears their hair long anymore, and all the best and brightest students have chestnut coloring. I know it doesn't make any sense, but it's the way things are. We've got to get you off to as good a start as possible. Don't you want to be a city girl?"

Katie stroked her hair, remembering when Clark had done the same thing. He wouldn't like it...but would that matter? She *did* want to belong to this world. She sucked in several breaths, wondering if this was why they had not chosen Allison with her wild, wiry, red hair.

She consented with a nod because her throat was too tight to speak, then sat herself down and refused to look into her reflection, instead watching the men again. Neil had shifted, hidden by the doorway, but she saw his arms fold over his chest. He swayed toward his father then away.

"Why can't Neil talk?" she asked.

The blades sliced through her hair.

"He's never spoken much," Mrs. Alcott said. "He didn't even cry much as a baby. He was always such a good boy. He'll warm up to you soon, don't worry. He's shy, but he has a good heart."

Katie said nothing because her throat was growing tighter with every snip of the scissors. Mrs. Alcott brought her hair forward, draping the blunt tips just over her shoulder.

"See?" the woman asked. "It's still long. We could go shorter though, if you want."

"No," Katie said.

"All right."

Mrs. Alcott reached for a bottle. She squirted brown foam into her hand and spread it through Katie's hair. "This won't stain your skin. It's formulated just for hair," she said. "Just rinse it out and use the shampoo. That's the box in the shower to the right. The left is body wash. If you want the water to be hotter or colder, just say 'hot' or 'cold,' but it should start at a comfortable temperature. There is a dress for you on that peg there. Just put your old dress in the corner, and we'll throw it out. The towels are in the warmer over there. Take your time."

Mrs. Alcott left, shutting the door behind her. Katie locked herself in before she dropped her head against her arm and tried not to cry. The foam's tiny bubbles popped against her forehead and there was nothing to do now except wash it back out.

Two feet of her hair lay discarded on the floor. She edged around it and shed her dress. The shower started as soon as she stepped in, the water spraying directly into her face and leaving her sputtering. So much water. Buckets of it, delivered steaming hot just like that. It felt wonderful, but the shower walls were glass and even with the door locked, she felt exposed.

She pressed all over the shampoo box, but nothing happened until she put her hand beneath the spout. A squirt of thick liquid piled into her palm. She washed and rinsed her hair with a vengeance, scrubbing until the water ran clear. She scoured her skin until it was red.

The water stopped as she stepped onto the cushioned mat. She lifted the lid of the warmer, pulled out the toasted towel, and dried as quickly as she could. The new dress was shorter than the ones at home, the hem ending an inch above her knee instead of falling comfortably to her calves. She tugged, but there was no lengthening it. It swished so high and loose that it felt like she was wearing only a shirt.

But it was beautiful, its material a vibrant blue, the neckline a tight V shape sporting a silver chain that stretched across her bare skin. Shoes were placed carefully underneath, little more than straps over a thick curved base. They made her taller, which she liked, but the pegs felt tacked on and offered no protection for anything that her feet may encounter.

She looked back into the mirror. A stranger with short brown hair stared back. She swallowed three times. She had to become a city girl now. No one at home would believe she was Katie.

Behind the Door

KATIE SAT ON THE BED, listening for the morning birds to tell her the time, knowing only that she had eaten dinner and slept, so now it should be the next day. There were pictures of city girls, posing in front of tall buildings stretching down long sidewalks or sitting at tables sipping from giant mugs. One girl sat on a bed with her legs crossed, wearing bright pink shoes and a pink dress, and holding her index finger against her lips. None of them had brown hair.

There were no mirrors, and she was glad. She kept her hair behind her shoulders, out of sight. She'd looked for her yellow dress, but it had vanished from the bathroom, along with her boots. Her spare dress, too, was missing from the crate.

A crystal bottle sat on the bed stand with lady slipper orchids etched in a winding pattern around the clear liquid. She picked it up, pressing the golden tip and the liquid spritzed out. It smelled like jasmine and something she couldn't identify, filling the air around her.

She pulled on the new shoes and practiced walking until she could put her feet in front of each other without wobbling. Then she opened the door to venture down the hallway, but the bedrooms showed nothing except darkness beneath the doors.

"It's better for sleeping," Mrs. Alcott had explained. "Even a small amount of light in a room interferes with your ability to make melatonin and keeps you from a deep, restorative sleep."

Katie's sleep hadn't been deep or restorative, though the bed was the softest place she'd ever laid and the air was chilled like a mild winter. It could have been the most luxurious night of her life, had not dreams of Clark marrying someone his father picked while she was gone plagued her sleep. She should have told him she planned to return, because Mr. Blackwell was sure to tell him that she wouldn't. Especially if all the men from the inborder were like Neil with his stony silence.

She wondered how she could befriend him, then shoved the idea away. Neil was like a Blackwell, viewing her through a biased lens that likely would never change. She was here to go to school and go to school she would. She'd done nothing to apologize for, so he'd just have to work through whatever he was feeling on his own.

Still, she slowed as true growls floated in from the living room and a voice she didn't recognize said, "Any rival's attempt to take over the pride is especially dangerous for young Amari. If his father is killed by the younger challenger, the first thing the new dominant lion will do is kill all the cubs."

There hadn't been a window the day before, but Katie stopped as a creature that looked a little like a mountain lion moved through the grass behind a large rectangle in the wall. She stepped back on instinct, then watched as the animal disappeared and reappeared, suddenly swimming through a river, like someone was flipping through photographs. Only they moved as the unknown man's voice continued to narrate.

"But the lion attempting to take over the pride is not the only danger threatening Amari and his mother. To escape across the river, he must avoid another enemy—the crocodile."

The moving photos continued to change, and Katie coaxed her breathing back into calm. Whatever it was, it wasn't real. But it looked real.

She crept into the living room, feeling her heart fall as she noted all seats were empty except for Neil's. At the right of the room, a counter separated the carpet from the tile, creating a short wall that guarded the kitchen. No one was in there, either.

Neil glanced toward her, then picked up a black rectangle. The creatures disappeared into darkness. The voice disappeared too, leaving silence to linger between them.

"Are your parents still asleep?" Katie asked.

Neil's eyes fell to his fingers as he picked at a loose thread on his pants. He took three breaths before he spoke one word in a deep tone. "Gone."

Katie's chin jutted forward. "When are they coming back?"

Neil shrugged. He stood and ambled past the counter to a white, upright case like the one Katie used to seal off the salt pork, but when he opened the door, a puff of cold air wafted toward her. He pulled out a black square container, put it into a white metal box, and hit a button that hurt her ears with a beep. The box's window lit up and the container began a slow spin.

Katie gripped the door frame, bracing herself for his anger, but Neil didn't seem mad today.

"Why can't you talk?" she asked.

He glared at her, yanked open the box, and pulled out the container. She almost expected him to toss it out the front door, but he plopped it in front of her and pulled back the clear paper on top.

The smell of bacon and eggs hit her nose. She stared at the rising steam as he dug into a drawer and sent a fork skidding across the counter toward her.

She caught it at the counter's edge. "Thanks."

She didn't hate the smell of bacon now. Suddenly, it smelled like home and made her heart ache. She sat on one of the stools, piercing the scrambled egg.

Neil leaned an arm on the counter and watched her.

She brought the egg to her mouth, chewed, caught the wince. The taste was vaguely familiar, but it was like chewing rubber.

"Hurts," Neil said.

"What does?" she asked.

His head tipped, though he kept his eyes on her.

"Oh. To talk?"

He nodded.

"Do you know why?"

He shook his head.

She tore the bacon into a small piece and tasted it gingerly. Less salt, and not as crispy but it tasted the same. "Well, maybe that's because you don't use it enough. Like muscles. The more you use them, the less they hurt when you do. I mean...within reason."

His eyes dropped and dulled.

She ate another mouthful of eggs. Wondered if Mrs. Alcott's assessment of her son's mental capacity was heavily blinded by motherly love. "Thanks for breakfast."

His eyes flickered back to her face and the corners of his mouth twitched and fell again to their stoic stance. She tried to think of yes or no questions.

"Do you go to the college too?"

His eyebrows dipped, and she couldn't tell if he was offended or confused, but he shook his head no.

"Are you...older than twenty?"

He gave a short nod, then held up two fingers.

"Twenty-two?"

Another nod.

"Do you have siblings?"

His head jerked backward, the eyebrows drawing deeper, and she amended. "Brothers or sisters?"

He blinked and shook his head.

"Are you leaving the house today too?"

His shoulders shrank and the dopey look returned. But he shook his head, slower now.

She wasn't sure when she was supposed to leave to be vaccinated or how to sign up for the school. But hunger had awakened, so she focused on finishing up the food. Neil leaned onto his forearm, content with silently staring.

She wished Clark was here.

"How'd the food get hot so fast?" she blurted before blushing, realizing he couldn't answer.

But he pointed to the smaller box.

"Well, I know that, but how does it light up? We have one of those at home, but it's never done anything," she said. "It belonged to my great-grandmother. We keep our sweet potatoes in it."

He tilted his head.

She shrugged. "Nothing happens when you hit the buttons at home. I swear everything in your house does something if you clap, or snap, or press a button."

He scanned the house, then walked to the doorway, glancing backward toward her. When she looked up, he disappeared, then peeked back in. After he disappeared a second time, she abandoned her meal to follow him. He led her up a flight of stairs to another central room that had doorways on each wall, one to the hallway and three to what looked to be bedrooms.

Rows of shelves held tiny structures, some created to look like miniature cars, some with scraggly bushes that created landscapes. Neil picked up a boat, holding it an inch from her nose. She scanned the tiny men that were glued to the bow of the ship.

She replaced confusion with a weak smile, wishing she'd finished her breakfast. "Did you make this?"

He nodded, then flung it back onto the shelf, spinning toward a castle that sat half-finished on a small table. Again glanced toward her, and again she followed.

Near the structure sat a sheet of pieces, all held captive in their molds. The castle was unfinished, though several pieces had been freed and painted. But four sailors had been moved from the ship into the castle, two near a table in the courtyard and two on the wall staring straight ahead.

"Um..." Katie faltered.

Neil sighed. Took one of the men from the wall, moved him to the drawbridge, and then spun the wheel until the board lifted to cover the gateway.

"I don't know what..."

He seized her wrist, almost yanked her to another scene, now a landscape with moss instead of bushes where large cats stalked brown and black animals that looked like striped deer. Neil's demeanor relaxed as he allowed her a glance, then moved to a different model in rapid succession. Never lingering over any except the castle, never moving any pieces. The rest of the sailors stayed put on their ship.

He flashed her a smile before his face returned to its neutral mask. He spun and headed down the stairs.

She followed slowly. "Where did your parents go?"

She should have waited to ask until he reached the bottom because all she caught of the reply was the back of his shoulders as he shrugged.

"Are they coming back today?"

Another shrug. He turned at the bottom into a door she hadn't noticed before. He punched a code into the panel next to it. The door opened without his aid and an acidic smell hit her, giving her an instant headache. They stepped onto a tile floor and her eyes fell on a rectangle hole, filled with clear water. Globe-shaped lights hung from the ceiling. Clear chairs, longer at the bottom than the top, rimmed the room. At the far corner, water cascaded down a pile of rocks into the rectangle like a spring.

"Is this where your water comes from?" she asked.

One side of his face scrunched but he shook his head, then set his palms together, one hand flat fingered, the other cupped. The cupped hand dove over his fingers toward the pool.

"Do you swim in that?" she asked.

He nodded and grinned, then pointed to her.

She shook her head. "No...not now." She wondered if it was deep enough to cover her head. She searched for fish, but there didn't seem to be any plants or creatures in it. "Is it just for swimming? We don't swim much where I come from."

His body sagged, eyes already falling away from her face to the water.

"The only water is at the river," Katie said. "And it's not good water. Sometimes it's safe, and there's lots of fish. Then we go in. But sometimes the fish die because something washes down from the inborder. If you get in the water and your legs are scratched, you can get infected. And if you drink it, you can die. So we don't swim much."

The story had gotten his attention, and his eyes pierced hers until she was finished. He eyed the water again, blinking, but then shrugged.

"I know there's no poison in here, probably, but..." She cut herself off, wishing she hadn't brought it up. He didn't need to know that she couldn't swim. Not until she trusted him. She glanced at the concrete walls, feeling choked by the stifling air.

"Do you want to go on a walk?" she asked.

He cocked his head like he didn't understand. Then he nodded slowly and pushed himself to his feet, walking to a machine on a platform at the far end of the room. He pressed a button, and the black path began to move.

She stared. "What is that?"

He stared back, then jumped onto the black strip, falling into a quick walk as the path moved beneath him and rolled under the machine. He took three strides that went nowhere, then stood until the machine carried him to the edge where he jumped off. He pointed toward her, then it.

"No, I mean a real walk," she stammered. "Outside. You could show me your city."

"Can't," he said.

"What?"

"Go out."

"Why not?"

"You're...here...now."

She eyed him, then strode down the hallway, past the couch, feeling her breath pick up but still felt like she was suffocating. She heard the door shut behind her, a beep, then his steps catching up.

She quickened her pace, swinging around the entryway and nearly hit the front door with her body. Grabbed the curved handle and yanked. A bolt caught the door from inside, only allowing the slightest rattle. She swallowed, feeling her throat begin to close. Fighting for air, she glanced for a number pad like he'd used, but there was nothing. She snapped, like Mrs. Alcott had done to open the drawers, but the door gave no response.

She used the last of her stored breath to ask, "What's the code?"

Silence behind her.

"Where's that black box your dad used to open it?" She yanked on the door again, looking for a button, a turning lock, a latch. But the handle was little more than a curved bar attached to the wood.

She turned. He watched her from the hall entrance with his hands tucked under his armpits.

A decorative steel square sat at the bottom and made her think of the door that Allison's dog came through. She pushed it with her foot, then tried to peel the top away, but it held fast.

"Neil!" she choked. "Open the door."

Back door. There was a back door. She bolted past him, shoving one side of his chest, though he hadn't actually blocked her way. Darted to the back door, only to find the same mocking handle. She shook it, but it didn't even rattle as she turned her eyes back toward the man.

"Neil, please. I need—I don't know how—the door."

Neil had only pivoted in place and was still staring at her from across the room. His eyes had widened, nostrils flaring like he, too, struggled to breathe.

She fought for calm, seeing her panic reflected in his eyes.

"How do you open the door?" she asked.

His eyes fell from her, searching the couch, the lamp that sat on the table beside it, then the air itself as his gaze traveled away from her. He swallowed. "You don't."

She yanked on the door, shouting, "Open this door!"

He took a step back, surprise flickering before his eyebrows began to quake. He glanced toward the corner of the ceiling again.

"Calm down. You're going to scare it." Clark's voice broke through the onslaught of panicked thoughts. Only Clark had been talking about a skunk they had come across in the woods, not a fully-grown man.

Katie's eyes followed Neil's attention, finding only another black circle the size of half an orange where the ceiling met two solid walls. Walls built to keep the family safe, that no one outside could break through—and no one inside could break out.

She stared at the man, who stared back, watching his broad shoulders hunch and his hands creep into his pockets.

A shrill sound pierced the silence.

She jumped, but his only reaction was a complete fall of his gaze to the floor. He walked to the counter that separated the living room from the kitchen. He picked up a curved white thing, connected by a spiraling tail to its base. Sucked in a second breath, then said in the polished tone he'd used the day before, "Yes?"

She heard another voice, the sharp consonants of ts, ds, and a c, but the words were muffled, like the night after the dance when Mayor Blackwell had berated Clark in an upstairs room while she stood on the street, realizing she should come back later. Only now, there was nowhere to go.

"How?" Neil asked.

He blinked at the answer.

Katie bolted for the bathroom, the only room in the house that had a lock, the only room where only one person was allowed. She jabbed it, heard its lock slide into place, and paced toward the shower where the water came from somewhere besides the rectangle pool.

"You can't let them know you're afraid." Clark's voice came again, this time talking about his own relatives.

She gripped her hair, pacing four lengths one way then the other.

The door rattled.

She grabbed the lid from the back of the toilet, hefting it, realizing even as she did that Neil was so tall, she'd only manage to smash his face if he did manage to get in. And then what? She'd still be locked in the house with him until his parents returned. He could easily hold her down, pick her up, move her anywhere he wanted...

She spied the shadow of his two feet appearing, first one than the other, under the crack of the door. She tightened her grip, tensing, waiting.

But the feet only rose and fell like a cat kneading the carpet. His voice was still deep, but it rasped around the edges again as he said, "Come out."

"No."

Silence. The feet didn't move.

"Come out," he tried again.

"No!"

The shadows shifted, first one than the other.

"We...can...watch...the lions."

Her eyebrows drew lower with each halting word, the first three spoken slowly, the last two as one.

She said nothing.

He panted. Rasped, "Please."

Her arms trembled beneath the weight of the toilet lid.

"Don't scare it," Clark said again.

She lowered her arms, eased the lid back onto its place.

Neil growled. She froze.

One of the shadows disappeared. A loud crack rattled the door.

She screamed, stumbling backward until her back hit the glass shower.

"Neil, if you come in here, I will bash your head in!"

The shrill noise returned, summoning Neil like a dog to a dinner bell.

She pressed her ear against the door, but he was too far to hear any words at all. In a few moments, a calmer voice floated down the hallway. Lions began to roar.

The Reward

SHE WOKE ON THE BATHROOM floor. Her shoulder ached, cushioned only by the shower mat. The towel, softer than any clothing she had at home, pressed against her cheek. She stared at the line of floor beneath the door and the dark edge of the breakfast container that blocked out the light beyond the crack.

The room smelled like soap, chemicals, and sausage. She shut her eyes again as her stomach growled, resisting the lifelong urge that had taught her whenever food was present, you ate as much as you could get. Twice yesterday, Neil had tried to bribe her with meals. The second time, it was all she could do to not open the door just long enough to slide the plate inside.

But she had gone days without food many times in her life. She had a water source right here. She even had the use of the toilet, a benefit she hadn't realized until last night. She could exist in this room until Mr. and Mrs. Alcott returned. Her eyes wandered up the slick walls to the tiny vent in the ceiling—the only opening in the room besides the door.

Exist. But not escape.

She curled her fingers into a fist, brought her knees close to her chest. Was she overreacting? Mrs. Alcott had said the house was built to keep them safe from the neighbors. Mr. Alcott had used something to open the door. Neil hadn't seemed angry in the morning. Were they locking her in or someone else out?

Either way. The door was locked, and the only way out was to figure out how to unlock it, hope that Mr. or Mrs. Alcott would, or convince Neil to show her how.

Her heart stirred, then slammed against her chest as Neil's feet plodded back across the carpet.

He'd used up the rich tones of his voice, retaining only a croak that hardly carried past the door. "I need in." Desperation rasped the edges of his voice, lending a feeble urgency to the tone. "Please."

The final word irked. She resisted rolling her eyes. She chose plan A: figure out how to unlock the door. Her legs felt like hardened stone, and she gasped as she stood, wobbling to the door.

She grasped the lock, closed her eyes. He hadn't hurt her so far, hadn't done anything more aggressive than kick the door. Her throat still pumped as she twisted the lock and stepped out, backing into the doorway of her bedroom.

Neil shoved a breakfast plate into her chest, spun himself around the edge of the bathroom door and closed it, leaving her standing alone. She heard a stream from inside, realized her window of time was short, and dropped the carton to dart to the front door. It was exactly as she remembered it, a smooth, immobile handle, good for nothing except pulling the door shut.

"Come on, come on, come on," she whispered. She searched the doorframe for a bar, a lock, a panel of buttons, anything. She clapped. Even jumped. Pushed and pulled. The only movable part seemed to be the metal square near the base, but it did little except wiggle beneath her prodding.

From the bathroom, she heard jets of water. She put her hands on her knees, blowing out a breath, searching for calm. He wasn't after her. He was taking a shower. He wasn't worried about her, which also meant he wasn't worried she'd escape.

She ran upstairs to the back rooms she hadn't been inside, peering at the ceilings, searching for a crawl space that might lead to an attic or out. But the air vents were small and square, too narrow for even her tiny frame to squeeze through.

She darted past the miniature houses, landscapes, and vehicles, into a bedroom as large as the kitchen at home, finding a massive bed and not much else. Paintings, lit from behind, cast a soft light across the room. One of them was an ocean view, glowing so that the sun looked red. She ripped it off the wall, finding only a cord running to tiny lights in the frame. She hung it up so quickly that it wobbled and fell with a crash as she ran to the next room.

And stopped, coming face to face with the same creature Neil had watched on the screen. It stood near the bed, one foot forward, mouth wide, teeth nearly the size of her finger. She gasped, choked back her scream. The lion stared back, frozen with one front paw in the air. She took a slow step back, then swayed forward. Blinked. Inched toward the creature. It watched the doorway behind her. No blinking eyes, no flickering ears, no sound coming from that gaping mouth.

But it was real.

She stepped closer, studying the hair around its neck. It was dead, but how had they kept its meat? Stuffed it? She watched the ribs, but they stayed still. Resisting all urge to snatch her own hand back, she reached out and touched the fur. Definitely real. Definitely dead. The glassy eyeball watched her, face forever pointed toward the doorway.

The same shrill ring from earlier came again, this time from a white machine next to the bed. Katie lifted the top part and held it to her ear as Neil had, but before she spoke, Neil's voice floated through the machine.

"Yes?"

Katie jumped as Mr. Alcott's voice came across the line. "AIDA notified me that you never turned in your work yesterday."

"The girl—"

"Is meant to be a reward for you, son, not a distraction."

"Mom—"

"You don't listen to what your mom says. You listen to what I say—shut up!—I'm talking, not you. You want to keep her?"

"Yes."

"Then you make sure you do your work, you understand?"

"Yes."

"What do you say?"

Silence.

Then the question was posted again in a sterner tone. "What do you say, Neil?"

"Sorry."

Katie sank onto the bed. Her hand fell to her lap as she stared at the wall. She'd never counted on Mr. Alcott for help, but panic flickered as memories clicked into place to incriminate Mrs. Alcott as well. They'd been the village and seen her. They'd smuggled her into their world. They'd changed her hair length and color. They'd promised to take her to school, and then they'd left. No one at home knew where she was. No one in the inborder even knew she was here. They'd chosen her, not Clark, not Allison. Not for a scholarship. For a reward.

She sucked in a slow breath and lifted the device back to her ear, but the men had finished talking. She returned it to its place, stood, and smoothed the wrinkled blanket to cover the evidence, feeling her hands already clumsy with a growing shake.

Her friends and family were hoping for a letter, but were they really expecting one? Would they assume she couldn't find a way to send it to the village? She'd been so determined to leave; would it shock anyone at all when she didn't return? It would be four years before anyone even expected her to. If they did realize something was wrong, even Clark couldn't get past the border to find her.

And then Neil was standing in the hallway behind her. She spun, stepping next to the creature like it would defend her. Neil stood, clad only from the waist down. His arms rippled like those of a baker, his hands hanging loosely at his side. His skin was so light it reflected the lamplight. She blushed, blinked, realizing even Clark, whose family managed three meals each day, shrank into an emaciated figure next to Neil.

Whatever, and whoever, this man was, she needed to ensure he didn't become her enemy. Right now, if his face was any sign, he had no dominant emotion beyond mild surprise at finding her in his bedroom.

"I'm sorry," she stammered, motioning toward the lion. "I saw him, and I thought...he was real. Alive, I mean." She stepped away from the lion and toward the man in the door, but he only inclined his head. "I'll leave your room," she sputtered, "if you'll let me."

He blinked, almost shaking himself from his own thoughts, if he had any. He stepped into the room, closer to her, but cleared the doorway.

His eyes lifted toward the corner of the room, then back at her. "Go wash."

Her stomach clenched so tightly it felt like her belly button met her spine. Don't make him an enemy.

She edged around him. "And then...we watch the lions?"

His eyes lit, head moving back an inch. Sparked with hope before it faded. "Later."

"Okay," she whispered and darted back down the hallway.

No way out, except through Neil. She shut herself in the bathroom again, putting her palms against the sink and gulping for air. Her mind tried out plans like they were new outfits, one after the other, each just as flimsy as the last. Whichever angle she took with him, she had to fully commit to the performance.

Nausea rose as Tucker's chitchat floated into her head.

"It'll be a lot different there for a nice girl like you. You're going to have to adapt."

She sucked in breath after breath, gripping the counter. Adapt. Win Neil over. Get him to unlock the door. He was her only hope.

The Gift

IF KATIE THOUGHT LIFE was slow in her village, here it was like trying to drizzle honey on a cold day. She unpacked her crate with the few items Mrs. Alcott hadn't taken, maintaining the facade of a girl who didn't know she was a reward. The Alcotts did not return that day or the day after. Neil did his work, ate, and watched the lions. He watched her too, but he usually looked away if she caught him.

There were no weapons in the house. Even the food in the containers was soft, easily cut with a table knife, and no sharp knives existed in the kitchen. There were glasses but no containers, no horns or flasks to carry water. She avoided the pool but used the walking machine. It was helpful to stay in shape, to force her pumping blood to match the thudding of her heart, but it was maddening to run so hard and far yet stay right where she'd started.

She had ripped the side of the extra pillow, creating a hiding spot for the things she would pilfer for her escape. She'd seen a candle in the living room that claimed to smell like cashmere and white amber—whatever that smelled like. They must have some way to light it, and she'd found a small match box in a drawer. It wasn't much, but it was *something*. She'd moved it into the kitchen to see if Neil would notice if items went missing.

He hadn't.

Her package from Clark sat on her bedside table, still concealed in wrinkled butcher paper and twine, its ragged presence ruining the pristine feel of the room. She hadn't wanted to open it, wanted it less now than ever. But when she woke and realized an entire week had passed since he'd given into her, she stretched across the bed to retrieve it, pulled the twine free, and carefully unfolded the paper.

A book.

She'd guessed it, but this book was new, still smelling of ink and fresh paper. She cracked the spine, spying a long list of words all beginning with the letter

'M' and all with their meaning coming just after. This wasn't from the school or even the Blackwell's tiny library.

She bit her lip, suddenly wondering if this had been purchased as a gift for Clark on the eve of his expected journey to the school in the city. Any gift from Mr. Blackwell, even for his own son, was nothing to sneeze at.

She peeked at the front pages. The title of the book was Dictionary, and the copyright was scarcely five years old. It must have cost Mr. Blackwell a year of well water payments. The pages smelled a little like hay and the distinct floral scent that emanated from the bowls of dried flower petals that sat around Clark's house. She buried her nose into the pages and let her face rest there, pretending to be in the entry hall to Clark's home.

Pain was a strange sensation. The material of her dress was softer than she'd ever felt, her elbows sank into the mattress, her body was relaxed, lacking its usual soreness. Yet pain came as an ebb and flow as she touched the book, as memories rose. Clark's face made her heart squeeze until she wiped all thoughts away.

Even if she hadn't been chosen as a captive, she still would be held at arm's length with Clark. All she had left was this book—and his handwriting. She blinked, seeing the indented lines of backward letters and turned the page to see his familiar script.

Katie,

You're going away. Probably forever. I'm not expecting you to come back, but I don't want you to leave still thinking I chose an inheritance over you. I'm sorry I dropped your hand. I didn't want to.

It's not the inheritance. It's our well. If my dad disowns me, I won't inherit the well. If I don't inherit the well, I can't control it. If I can't control it, I have to stand by and keep watching my family demand payment for water.

When your parents died from drinking the river water, it almost killed me. That is why I can't bring you into my life yet. It's not because I don't want you there. That's why I asked you if you would be willing to wait in secret, but not forever. But now you are going away. I want to stop you, but I won't.

Clark

P. S. I hope you find everything you ever wanted.

She flung the book aside, burying her face into the blankets so Neil didn't hear her sob. She hadn't found anything she'd wanted. No scholarship, no school, no chance to become a polished, educated woman. Was the scholarship even real or was it some kind of filter to find a girl who was naive enough to believe someone had seen something of worth in her?

She pulled her knees in closer and glared at the women on the wall. She couldn't live the rest of her life here. She racked her memories for something to cling to, some time she'd come up with a resourceful solution when all seemed lost. But she had none. Every time she'd ever been in a jam, someone had come along and helped her.

Clark had let her drink his water. Allison had mouthed a missing answer. Her father had used the sleeves from his only shirt to bind her ankle when she'd sprained it. Even Mallory and Jeremy had prepared to open their home to her. And what had she done for them, beside leave without so much as committing to their request to write? Not much. But she would.

If the scholarship was real, she'd find her own way to the school. If it wasn't...she had to warn the village before it happened again and someone else ended up locked inside a windowless, government-issued house.

She traced Clark's handwriting, pushed herself off the bed to busy herself with the only thing that gave any sort of normalcy or rhythm to her days. She still had no plan, but the more she ate, the stronger she would be for when she did.

She eyed Neil, who glanced back from his place on the couch. He spent most of his time there, apparently doing the work he was required to turn in every day. It mostly consisted of typing series of numbers that created images on the same screen where the lions roamed. It was fascinating to watch shapes fill with color and texture, eventually forming layers of art that created scenic worlds. But she hadn't figured out what they were for or what happened to them once they were finished. Neil never looked at his old work and didn't seem to care what happened to it as long as it was uploaded by dinner.

It was weird though, how he could glance over, even watch her pass through the room without ever stalling the clatter of his fingers on the keyboard. She passed him, opened the door, and counted the containers. Only four left.

"Neil?" she asked. "Will your parents come back before the food runs out?"

He shrugged with a calmness that baffled her. But food had to come in sometime, and it couldn't pass through walls.

"How do you get more food when it runs out?"

He pointed toward the tin square on the front door. She glanced at it, then moved out of his sight to put the food into the tiny oven. Her hands shook. So the little square did open...somehow. A human must physically carry the groceries to bring them; someone would be on the other side of the door when it opened. If she couldn't fit through, maybe a piece of paper could.

The machine behind her beeped. She seized the opportunity for conversation as she began to warm the first carton of food. "Neil, what do you call the beeping box?"

It took him so many seconds to answer that she began to think that he wouldn't, but suddenly he hovered near the doorway.

"Microwave," he said.

She scrunched her nose. "A microwave of...heat?"

He shrugged.

"Y'all have weird names for things."

He grinned. "Pitchfork."

"That's not weird."

He wagged his head.

"Okay, it's a little weird. Not as weird as an oven called "tiny waves." She saw him grin and ventured carefully, "So, will these groceries be delivered before we run out of food in that...what's that called?"

"Refrigerator," he answered, then swallowed before he continued, "One box...each...meal."

"Then more comes?"

He nodded.

The microwave beeped, and she pulled the first carton out, sliding it across the counter toward him. He caught it, sent her another grin, and pulled the lid off. She put her portion inside and started the timer again.

"What if the crops fail?"

"Hmm?"

"If the farmers don't bring food. Y'all don't store anything ahead?"

He shrugged again. "Never...ran out."

She frowned. "We have."

Neil picked up his portion and motioned her to the couch. "Of food?"

"Yeah. Especially at the beginning of spring. You have to stop eating the grain or you'll have nothing to plant, but there's not a lot of crops producing yet. We'll still have salted meat, but you have to look for dandelions and chickweed or you'll get sick. I guess they store it here better because of...ridged-ators." His mouth curled up, eyes sparkling, and she amended, "What'd you call it?"

"Refrigerator," he said, the coughed. "Who's 'we'?"

"Mallory and me. My sister."

He blinked. "I thought...you're alone."

"No." She pulled the container free and settled in, watching him carefully as she spoke. "I have a sister and a brother-in-law. They were so excited for me to come to school. They made me promise to write and tell them all about it."

Neil's face broke into a thousand tiny lines, before he lifted his eyebrows back into their place.

"Did you know I'll be going to school?" she asked. "I got a scholarship for college."

Neil reached for the remote. He hit the button, and the lions appeared again.

"This...your village?" he asked.

"Uh, no," she said. "That doesn't look like where I come from. But there are lots of other places in the world. I saw them on an old map."

"Other places...here too," he said. "But...I like...the lions."

She finished her meal and lay with her head in her elbow, watching two male lions wrestle, their claws slashing trails of torn flesh. But Neil's attention outlasted hers, and after they'd finished fighting and the lady lions were pulling apart a gazelle, she retrieved Clark's dictionary from her room. She would rather read there, but she forced herself to return to the couch.

Neil sent a surprised flicker of a smile as she settled next to him. He turned his attention to the animals, only moving his eyes in response to the changing images. She could still see the lions' tiny reflections in his pupils, noticed the red blood vessels bursting through the white rims. Perhaps he watched without seeing, the way her eyes scanned lines of words without comprehension. Perhaps he watched to avoid his own thoughts. She knew only that he didn't look away until one lion had run away, leaving the lone victor to return to his pride.

The show turned back to the grazing gazelles—gazelle scenes rarely ended happily—and she returned her eyes to the page, flipping idly through and careful not to show Clark's handwriting.

She heard the soft crackle of a swallow. The rush of air through his nostrils. The dry pop as his lips parted, all in a second. Then he spoke.

"I'll protect you."

She froze, page mid-turn, cocked her head only enough to see that he still studied the screen. "From what?"

His pupils fell, roved as though they were searching for a pile of words scattered on the table, choosing them as carefully as currency. He blinked twice. Pulled in another breath. "Anything."

The Plan

"I'LL PROTECT YOU...from anything."

His words had echoed through her head, following her into her dreams. She'd woke gasping, afterimages still dancing across the wall: the door finally yielding to her yank, but before she could step out, snakes had begun to slither inside. Neil had stomped on their heads, slamming the door again, but his eyes had widened as he turned to her. She'd glance down, finding fangs dug into her arm, ten rattlesnakes dangling from her flesh. She'd woken herself shaking her arm and the snakes had vanished. If only the memory of the dream had too.

She pushed the blankets back and grabbed an unworn dress on the way to the bathroom. The hot water appeared at her summons. She eyed the spout through the swirling steam, imagining crawling through it to freedom. She'd lost count of the days. It seemed she'd been here forever, though if she guessed, she thought it was somewhere between three and four weeks. Too long to convince herself that there had been a misunderstanding, and the Alcotts still intended to help her begin school.

There were only four meals left, which meant they would eat tonight, breakfast tomorrow, and before noon, someone would be at the door. She had to make sure she was ready on the inside when it opened.

She'd torn a page from the back of the dictionary, used her only pencil from home to write a message. The door would open. She'd drop it through. Someone would read it. Someone would help.

But none of her clothing had pockets and there was nothing near the door to conceal a note. Neil could see the entryway from his usual spot on the couch. He could ruin her entire plan.

Promises of protection didn't matter when he still wouldn't open the door for her. Of course he was going to protect her. She was his reward.

She rubbed her eyes, running various scenarios over and over in her mind and finding problems with all of them. There was no excuse for her to go into the entryway, so she wouldn't be able to wait in it. But she needed to stay near enough to dart to the little door when it opened.

She stared into the fogging glass walls of the shower, blinking out of her thoughts as faded letters began to form on the glass.

LIONS.

She stepped from beneath the spray. "Hotter," she told the pipe. It responded, burning the edges of her toes. Steam rose around her, outlining the message on the glass.

THEY WATCH US LIKE THE LIONS.

Her throat made a grunting noise. She stood stunned, before she rubbed out the message, leaped onto the rug she'd slept on weeks before, dried and dressed faster than she ever had on the cold days at home.

She stood clutching the damp towel to her chest.

They watch us...

The sailors standing on the corner of the castle wall: two people watching two people.

She heard the narrator's voice describing the lions' habits, every hunt analyzed, every roar overheard.

But how? There were no other people in the house, no windows. And if they could somehow see what happened in the bathroom, why had Neil risked leaving her a message?

Unless they couldn't. Was that why Mrs. Alcott had insisted that this was a private room, that only one person could be in this room at a time? Was she the one watching?

Blood began to drain from Katie's face, but the mirror was too fogged to see her reflection. She swallowed. Brought a shaking finger to the mirror over the sink to write.

Am I allowed to leave?

Her stomach churned. She glanced back to the shower where all evidence of communication had been wiped clean. Lifted her finger again, placing it just beneath the question.

Are YOU allowed to leave?

Panic rose, and she pushed it down. Neil had said that he didn't open the doors, not that he wouldn't open them. What if he *couldn't* open them? But how could anyone be watching anything that happened in a house with no windows? There was no one here except him and her. He must be lying. But why would he lie?

She shook her head, then opened her eyes. The lions. Could the box that summoned the lions somehow summon them, showing them in another living room? That box was on the wall facing away from the entryway, so no one would be able to see her there. There was nothing in the entryway except two solid walls, the side table, and the door. She could still pull off her plan. But if someone came to rescue her, would they actually be rescuing Neil too?

She pushed the thought away. Neil was a wildcard she couldn't afford to play. Besides, he'd shown no protest to his captivity—if it was one. Captive or not, he couldn't witness her slip the note out of the door.

But he'd be in the living room working on the screen unless the delivery came early in the morning while he was asleep. Or unless he was *still* asleep. She smiled as the missing part of the plan fell into place. If Neil needed to get his work done and didn't during the day, he'd just have to stay up late to do it.

She nodded at her mirrored accomplice, a manipulative girl she was recognizing less and less. Then walked down the hall to make their second-to-last meals. They were nearly out of coffee too. She emptied the canister, washing the grounds down the drain. Brought her treacherous offering to the couch and, as Neil began to eat, she began to share stories of home.

Neil's eyes traveled between his food and her face, intrigue growing into something close to a rapt attention that only faded whenever he glanced at the clock. She nearly lost him, but when he began to fill out the leaves on a screen-tree, she kept the chatter going, finding anything familiar to point out that looked like her world.

Could he add birds to the tree? One time, a bird fell out of a tree and Katherine climbed it and got the bird safely inside the nest, but she fell on the way down and couldn't move for thirty minutes, and Katie thought she might be paralyzed forever but she wasn't. And Clark had come along on his horse and given Katherine a ride home and let Katie walk beside him and hold the second rein, and that's when they first started talking outside of school.

Her stories came with few pauses and fewer breaths, but it was Neil's fingers that grew sluggish. She continued the stories until he set the keyboard to the side, pulled up his feet on the cushion, and turned to face her.

Victory. Except her voice began to sound as ragged as his, and when she began croaking, he turned back to the screen.

She swallowed dryly but managed to ask a quick question. "Can we watch the lions?"

He stared and, for a moment, she'd worried she'd given herself away. But his mouth tipped upward, and he pressed the button again. If anyone was watching them, she was the best companion they could have ever picked. She inched closer to Neil, careful not to touch him, and forced herself to smile as he brought the horrid creatures to life.

The Chance

KATIE'S STEPS BETRAYED her with a soft noise as she peeled her sweaty heels from the white stone tile. The LED lights of the clock read 11:29 a.m. Her eyes darted toward the couch, where Neil had sat up nearly all night and eventually crashed. He looked younger now, his chest rising and falling with the slow breath of sleep.

Her fingers tightened against the folded square of paper. She winced as it crinkled. Twelve steps would carry her to the front door, their sound hopefully covered by the mechanical grind of the gears as it opened for the delivery.

She rehearsed the process as she stepped through the arched entryway, expecting a short window when she could drop the message onto the shelf without it sliding into the grocery sack. A few seconds to tell a stranger that she was here. A few seconds to escape to freedom.

Neil sucked in a sharp breath, his arm lifted a few inches, then slowly lowered back to his chest. He shifted, rolled his head to one side, and fell back into a deep sleep.

Katie swallowed. Hesitated. If this worked, what would happen to—

It doesn't matter! He made his bed; he lays in it.

The gears buzzed, the door rising to allow an inside shelf to unfold. A bag appeared, held by dark brown fingertips. She dashed to the door, biting back the urge to yell. The shelf tilted until the bag fell with a thud, then groaned as it straightened back into place. She heard the shuffle of shoes as the delivery man stepped back. She tossed the paper through the gap. It landed on the shelf, sliding off into the sunlight just before the top edge made a complete halt. The doors lowered again, the hinges grinding into their locked position on either side of the shelf.

So simple. So slow. She'd succeeded but the entire process had been so methodical and short, it hardly felt like anything extraordinary. She held her breath, closed her eyes, listened for any movement on the other side of the door.

He had to have seen it. He must be reading it now. He'd get the police, they'd break down the door, and that was that.

She'd be free, and she hadn't any help this time. Maybe the police would even take her home. She could see her sister as early as tonight. And Clark.

She smiled.

A shrill scream pierced from the machine on the table. Neil groaned, reaching for the talking machine again. She glanced toward the TV, but it was still hidden, still facing the opposite wall. It couldn't see her, surely. But Neil could. Katie snatched the grocery bag, forcing herself onto shaking legs.

"Yes?" Neil's answer rasped so badly, he had to try a second time. "Yes?"

Mr. Alcott shouted so loudly that Katie could hear bits of words from the entryway.

"Shh!" Neil hissed. He turned his face quickly toward the hallway, glancing toward Katie's bedroom.

Katie clutched the paper sack The grocery man must have seen the note. He could be reading it in his truck right now.

Neil stiffened, turning to stare at her.

"I was just...getting the groceries," she stammered.

His face slacked. His jaw gaped. He slammed the earpiece down, then rose to roar. "What did—?" His shout turned into a choked cough.

"Nothing! I didn't..."

He surged toward her, grabbing her shoulders, his fingers digging into the soft points beneath her collar bones. He slammed her against the door. The bag fell, the brown paper splitting and spilling out a sliding tower of stacked containers. She screamed as loudly as she could.

His paw clamped over her mouth, cutting off the sound. "Shh!" he hissed, spinning her against his chest. "Shh!"

He lifted her. She kicked the air between his legs, only landing one good blow to his shin. She writhed as he carried her past the living room, down the hall into her room where the city girls smirked from the walls. She felt herself launch, flailed midair, put her arms out to break her fall, and landed so hard that the blanket pooled around her fingers as she slid forward.

Neil spun, gripping his head. He strode to the wall, punching it in rapid succession, leaving three deep dents.

A second scream clawed its way up Katie's throat, breaking loose in a hoarse sob.

Neil spun, clamped his hand back over her mouth, pushing the back of her head into the mattress. "Don't! Shh!"

His hand snaked upward until the edge of his palm blocked her nose and mouth, turning the piercing sound into little more than a bottled-up whimper. The air went back into her lungs, trapped and stale. She grabbed his arm, digging her nails into his skin, but he only pushed harder.

Blackness hovered at the edge of her vision, a friend offering to swoop in and carry her into oblivion. She clawed at his fingers, trying to pry his grip loose.

He tightened them. "Shh!" he hissed again. "Shh!"

Tears furrowed into a river that pooled into her hair. She stopped struggling. Nodded.

"Don't scream," he said.

She nodded again as the blackness closed in.

Neil lifted his hand. He sat back as she gasped, drawing in air, cool, saturated with the sharp tang of all the things she'd never smelled before she'd stepped into this house. The breath brought its own noise, a stifled sob as her mind flew down the hallway and slammed into the door, still closed, still locked.

She rolled, pushed her hands beneath her but her arms collapsed, leaving her shaking too hard to do anything besides curl into a ball. But Neil didn't move. She could hear him sucking in his own strangled breaths. She peeked at him, but his rage had drained into something close to stunned curiosity.

He twisted his hand to study the side of his palm where her tears coated the bruise on his smallest finger. He curled his fingers, watching the drop run down his wrist and looked back to her face. He blinked. Then backed toward the edge of the bed, unfolded his long legs, and strode out the door.

She sucked in breath after breath, too numb to run. The doors were locked. She'd starve in the bathroom, couldn't lock the kitchen. She couldn't even fight Neil off, which left the man free to do whatever he wanted to her. She rolled onto her side, away from the door, fighting the urge to breathe too much now that she could breathe at all.

Stupid. Stupid for coming here. Stupid for believing even for a moment, that she'd been chosen for a scholarship over the others from her village. Stupid for not questioning why, not running back to Tucker instead of curling compliantly onto a floorboard, stupid for expecting that a random delivery man would become her salvation. Just stupid.

She felt the bed sink like Neal had crawled back onto it. She scrunched her eyes tighter, feeling her breath quickening. She waited, but he didn't move again.

"Here," Neil said.

The smell of water coaxed her to open her eyes, and she saw only a clear glass hovering in front of her face.

She pushed herself shakily onto her forearm. He held out the glass in one hand and a small white oval in the other. She wiped her eyes, took the glass, peeking toward the oval.

He swallowed, like he was trying to wet his own throat, then glanced at the wet line on his arm as he said, "I make those too."

"Tears?" she asked.

He nodded, then shoved the white oval toward her.

"I don't know what that is," she said.

His eyes roved the gift. "Stops tears."

She sighed, wondering if Neil knew how many stupid lies she'd believed from his parents. If he knew the foolishness of eating something you didn't know. If it would harm her.

She took the oval.

"Swallow," he said. "Don't chew."

Maybe it would kill her. The thought came with a tinge of hope. She set it onto her tongue, wincing at the bitter taste, then washed it down with the water.

Satisfied, Neil took away the glass and lowered himself beside her, watching her face. Feeling defiant, she kept the eye contact, willing him to look away. But he only watched her with the unblinking stare of a cat.

He frowned, like he was searching for words. "You won't...leave."

Whatever the white oval was supposed to do, it didn't dry up her tears. She felt them trickle as she watched Neil. Decided he was killing her and decided she didn't care. She couldn't read his thoughts, but she saw their calculation.

Then he nodded and closed his eyes. After a moment, his slow breath brushed her face as it smoothed into sleep.

Her thoughts began to wander, the pain in her head dissipating, feeling like she was floating. Then blackness embraced her.

The Protector

A DOOR SLAMMED. KATIE woke at the same time as Neil. Their eyes met, exchanging confusion, realization, then panic as the voices rose. Shouts and pleas mingled in nonsensical sentences that jumbled as they carried down the hall.

Neil rolled off the bed, lifting his eyes toward the door. Katie scrambled onto the carpet, her mind supplying only one clear thought: the door had opened for three seconds, and she'd missed it.

Mrs. Alcott's pleas grew louder. "...was going so well."

Neil glanced at the three holes he'd punched into the wall. He grabbed Katie's hand, dragging her from the room.

As they passed the bathroom door, she cast a worried glance at the message hidden in the mirror. There was no time to erase it now. The Alcotts met them at the beginning of the hallway. Mrs. Alcott hovered behind her husband, clutching her purse.

Mr. Alcott didn't pause his stride until his nose stopped two inches from Neil's eyes. "You want her or not?"

"Richard..." Mrs. Alcott murmured behind him.

"I can take her right now."

Neil reached for Katie's hand, his fingers crushing hers.

Mr. Alcott pointed to the couch and roared, "Sit!"

Katie stepped toward Neil, startling even herself, feeling numbness wash over her as he tugged her to the couch.

Mr. Alcott glared as he held up a folded paper. Katie's heart slowed as he slowly opened it to read, "I am from the village of Blackwood. My name is Katie Hunter. My sister is Mallory Huddleston, wife of Jeremy Huddleston. Please help me. I was tricked and locked inside this house. There is a man who won't let me out." He folded the note, eyeing her. "Congratulations, Katie Hunter. We came to let you out."

"Richard..." Mrs. Alcott tried again.

Neil's eyes rose. "She's mine."

"She betrayed you, son!"

"Gift."

The silence stiffened the air between them. Richard took a breath. "AIDA, what is Neil's score for this week?"

A disembodied voice floated from the corner of the room. "Neil's behavior score has fallen twenty points this week, making his current score a seventy-seven."

"Play all highlights for Neil from this week."

The screen in the living room flickered to life. Katie stared as Neil's form appeared on the screen, at all angles, in all rooms, one after another, as though she was looking through eyes stationed at every corner.

A montage of moments flashed by; some she remembered like Neil kicking the bathroom door, slamming her in the entrance, hitting the wall. Some she didn't: Neil dropping a glass in the kitchen, cursing as his keyboard slipped, pacing the house as the numbers 11:45 p.m. flashed onto the screen. Others she didn't even understand. Moments when he sat with the keyboard in his lap staring at the wall, taking food from the refrigerator, answering Mr. Alcott's summons on the second shrill ring, then red words that flashed.

Tuesday submission: Incomplete

Friday submission: Late

The callous voice spoke again. "Neil's emotions peaked at rage, thirty points above the recommended stage. His production fell by fifteen percent with two days of overdue assignments. He displayed the beginning stages of bad habits, such as sleep deprivation, procrastination, and work negligence. He engaged in advanced stages of violence. He continues to engage in previous bad behaviors such as eating more than the recommended portions, delayed responses to the telephone, and evading my cameras. This completes my current highlight reel for this week. Do you want me to engage in correction mode?"

"No, AIDA. Do not engage in correction mode." Mr. Alcott turned stony eyes back onto Neil. "I expect that by this time next week, your score will return to at least a ninety-eight and any correction moments will be accidental."

Neil swallowed, keeping his attention on the wall ahead. "Yes."

"This girl is like a pet, Neil. If you insist on keeping her, you are responsible for her. If you can't keep her under control, she cannot stay."

Katie gripped her knees, torn between standing to yell and making herself as small as possible. Neil's eyes turned toward her. Doubt crept into them, but he opened his mouth.

"Before you answer..." Mr. Alcott said quickly, "AIDA, play all highlight moments for Katie this week."

Now it was Katie on the screen. Yanking on the front door, running to the back, yelling at Neil to open the door, leaving her bed unmade. A shot of the hallway showed her plate sitting untouched outside the bathroom door. A shot of her laughing while working on the models with Neil, which zoomed in as he turned away and her face fell into a forlorn look. Crying into her pillow at night. Ripping that same pillow to create her hiding place.

Were no moments safe from this creature? Katie's stomach grew tighter and tighter as she watched herself sneaking past Neil with the note. Watched the real Neil's face empty of all color as he witnessed her full betrayal.

She gritted her teeth as AIDA's voice carried across the speaker: "Katie's behavior baseline is at an eighty-six according to an average city woman and an eleven according to a laborer. Her emotional level peaked at guilt. Katie displayed undesirable baseline habits such as sloppiness, door slamming, raising her voice, and sporadic meal intakes. She engaged in contradictory behavior, such as conflicting statements and displayed physical cues that indicate deception. Reportable behavior includes attempts at breaching the front and back door and attempts to engage with visitors. This completes the highlight reel for Katie for this week. Correction mode is not available for Katie. Do you want me to sync?"

"No," Mr. Alcott answered.

His voice floated around Katie, distant as though her mind had fled the room that trapped her body. She heard Mrs. Alcott murmur something.

"AIDA, off," Mr. Alcott said. He waited for a beep before he faced Neil. "We are leaving again today. We came back to handle this, but I'm speaking at a conference first thing in the morning. If you want Katie, you're going to have to keep her under control."

Neil clenched his jaw, looking at the space beyond his father. He gave a grim nod.

"Katie." Mr. Alcott turned toward her. He held up the paper. "Let me tell you about girls like you. Girls like you who come to the inborder usually come to work. If you were next door, you'd be doing all the chores, you'd be wearing one outfit every day, and you would never speak to anyone except for 'yes sir' or 'yes ma'am.' If you *did* manage to get this letter to the grocery man or break your way out and run to a neighbor's house, they'd return you to me or put you to work in their own home."

"But it's different with us," Mrs. Alcott spoke up. "You're not a captive, not really. You're a companion."

"We brought you for Neil," Mr. Alcott said. "You belong to him. If you are good to him, we will be good to you. But make no mistake. You will never be going home, but we can replace you in an instant."

Head still swimming, Katie sneaked a glance toward Neil, but his eyes were trained on his knee and only his thumb moved to rub it. A cold wave swept over her head, down her body, leaving even her insides numb. She swallowed, then nodded, her throat too tight to speak.

Mr. Alcott frowned but released his glare, turning it back onto his son. "You still want her?"

Neil's face blanked, though his thumb increased in speed as he rubbed it against his knee. He gave a short nod.

"Are you sure?"

Neil swallowed. His fingers tightened on his knee. He nodded again.

"All right." Mr. Alcott's voice rose in a dismissive tone that didn't cover his displeasure. He glanced at Mrs. Alcott as he dug the black rectangle from his pocket and spoke into it. "Turn on AIDA."

A beeping sound responded before AIDA answered, "Hello, Mr. Alcott. How can I serve you?"

"AIDA, engage in correction mode one," Mr. Alcott said.

Neil's spine straightened as his chin jerked up. He glared toward his father.

"Your mother and I are expected to be on a red-eye flight, which only gives us a few hours to get this under control," the man said. "Before we go, what do you say?"

Neil swallowed, said nothing.

"Rich..." Mrs. Alcott murmured before she pressed her own lips together and fidgeted with her purse.

Neil's chest rose with a shallow breath before he replied, "Sorry." Two syllables, spoken softly, quickly.

He blinked. Then jolted, almost jumping in his seat, squeezing his eyes shut.

"AIDA, engage in correction mode two," Mr. Alcott replied.

A soft whimper followed Neil's swallow. Mrs. Alcott turned her face to the side, studying the painting to her left. Katie stared, her mind feebly working to make sense of what she was witnessing.

"Again," Mr. Alcott said.

Neil's breath picked up. His face flushed from white to red. A slight cough. Then he said, "Sorry." Again, the brace, again his body hunched forward like an invisible fist hit his middle. His hand clawed the base of his throat like he was tearing something away.

"AIDA, engage in correction mode three."

The command drained Neil's air with a half-whispered, "No."

"Yes," Mr. Alcott answered. "Again."

Again, the word. Again, the reaction, only this time Neil rocked three times after the jolt. He stayed down for a moment, his ribs draped across his knees.

"What are you doing?" Katie sputtered. "Why are you doing that?"

"I don't know how your world works, Katie," Mr. Alcott answered. "But here, there are consequences for people who fail to perform their roles."

Consequences she understood, but this was more akin to magical torture. "*How* are you doing that?"

Mr. Alcott gave no reply.

Neil sat up again. A tear trailed down the sharp bone of his cheek.

Mr. Alcott waited until it dripped off Neil's chin before he said, "AIDA, engage in correction mode four."

"Richard!" Mrs. Alcott scolded. "He won't be able to speak to Katie."

Neil's eyes filled with a fresh flood but dimmed like the light fading from a dying animal.

"Neil, take Katie's hand."

Neil's forehead bunched into pleading.

"Take her hand, so she understands what her choices are doing to you."

Neil glared, gave a short shake of his head.

Mr. Alcott's eyebrows climbed. "Should we move on to level five? This isn't going to stop until you take her hand, but I don't care what level that happens on. Shake your head again, and we can go all the way to ten if you want."

"Richard, ten could kill him!" Mrs. Alcott scolded.

Katie grabbed Neil's hand. He turned a surprised face toward her. A second tear leaked from one of his eyes. Too afraid to speak again, she gave the same sort of halfhearted encouraging nod that Mallory had so often given her.

His hand was hot. His palm was trembling, the muscles twitching their own rhythm. In her peripheral vision, she saw Mrs. Alcott's hand move to her chest.

Neil swallowed, glanced toward the man who towered over them, then looked back at her like he was directing the word toward her. His voice resonated like the deeper tone was still trying to squeeze between his rasps. "I'm sorry."

Nothing happened.

She stared, blinked twice, and began to speak.

The stinging burn hit her fingertips, almost instantly spreading through her body, creating responses she had no control over. Her toes scrunched in her shoes, her fingers curled in themselves, her calf muscles knotted, like her body itself had gripped her. She tried to let go, but her hand was cemented against his. The sensation, though almost instant, seemed to last forever before it released her, only to replace the tightness with a stinging heat that knocked her back.

Freed now, her arms and legs moved on their own accord, all four limbs flailing beneath her to crawl backward, over the arm of the couch, until she fell into a curled position on the floor. She stayed on the floor as Mr. Alcott took the level up to five, squeezing her eyes like somehow if she couldn't see something, it wouldn't happen.

The Compromise

KATIE SAT WITH HER hands folded in her lap, feet huddled together like they sought comfort from each other. Gloriously numb, except the distant pain of the hairbrush being drawn through her hair in fast, repetitive strokes.

"Things aren't really as bad as they seem," Mrs. Alcott said. "You have seen Richard at his worst, but this *is* his worst. You haven't had a chance at all to see him when he's in a good mood."

Katie didn't want to think about Mr. Alcott or what it would take to transform him into someone besides the grim-faced man looming over them, unmoved by his own son's pain.

"Who is AIDA?" Katie asked.

"Oh, she's not anybody," Mrs. Alcott said. "It's not a name. It's an acronym. AIDA stands for 'artificially intelligent domestic aid.' She's supposed to do things like listen for your grocery list, turn lights off and on, and keep people from breaking into the house. She films all your life moments too. Then she'll compile all the good moments, so you have them to look back on. The correction mode was an add-on that Richard invented for the prison system."

Katie swallowed, aware that AIDA was still watching, still recording everything she asked, "But...how does she punish Neil?"

"He's got a bit of metal in his neck. A chip," Mrs. Alcott said. "She's synced to it."

"Do *you* have a chip?"

"Of course not." Mrs. Alcott parted Katie's hair into three sections and flipped the ends over each other, one after the other. "Neil's was a prototype. Richard needed to test it out, you see. I suppose I could have let him insert it into me, but he was set on installing it into Neil. It was...well, he hadn't programmed AIDA with the correction mode. That came later when Neil turned six."

"Does he get punished a lot? Is that why he can't talk?"

"Oh no!" The woman's hands jumped, giving Katie's hair an accidental jerk. "No, this rarely happens. Neil's usually very compliant. Richard was trying to scare you. Neil's just out of the habit of talking. Most of the time he's got no one to talk to. Richard gets jealous, you know, if I talk to Neil too much. That's why I found you." The braiding slowed as Mrs. Alcott looked into the mirror like it was showing her former days. "But he did used to sing sometimes. He had the sweetest little voice. I never hear him sing anymore, not even through AIDA when he's alone. His voice is nice when he does talk, though. Don't you think he has a pleasant voice?"

"I haven't heard very much of it," she said. Accusation crept into her tone.

"You will. He'll warm up to you. He just needs some time. You must realize that Neil hasn't really been around a girl, so you're going to have to nudge him a bit. But he's a quick learner, so it's really an ideal situation for you. He's eager to please you. He just hasn't quite figured out how."

Katie gripped her hands, cutting the woman off with a question. "Can't you turn the correction mode off?"

"AIDA is synced with Mr. Alcott's voice. She only responds to him." The woman paused to rub her eye. "I can help though, in my own little way. I'm sure he'll take away the restrictions on Neil soon. But much of that will be based on you, Katie. Richard needs to see that you're happy living here at the house, and that you'll not try to run away again."

Katie bit hard on her tongue, locking her tears and feeling her nose prick in response.

"Katie," the woman's voice became clipped. "You are being offered a life of luxury without even having to work for it. Neil works, you're his companion, and Mr. Alcott and I provide you both with everything you need. That is a generous deal, better than anything you would have ever gotten in your village and certainly better than the alternative if you insist on trying to leave. If you would put as much effort into enjoying your circumstances instead of leaving them, you could have a very good life here."

And if she didn't, she might get a chip too. Katie gagged. "Okay."

"Okay?" Mrs. Alcott asked, surprised.

"Okay."

She heard the breath seep through the woman's lips. Material brushed with a sudden shift as the woman reached for a hair tie.

"I know what you're feeling, Katie," Mrs. Alcott said. "I was chosen, too, for Mr. Alcott. We saw each other, sometimes, at social functions. His parents knew mine. I'd hardly ever spoken to him before we married. But I made it my business to find all the things that pleased him, like a little game. It was fun—and now he can't get along without me. Of course, it's a little harder for you since you have to please Neil and Richard, but once Richard sees you happy and Neil bonding with you, he'll relax. That's all he really wants, you know, for Neil to be happy, because then Neil does his work better."

"You mean building the worlds on the screens?"

"Um-hum. That is Neil's job. And your job is to make him happy."

Making Neil happy. Even if the role was assigned to her, even if she only accepted it for survival, it was no longer a complete fabrication, a tactical maneuver. It was just expected. By everyone.

"Okay," she said again.

"Good." Mrs. Alcott reached for her handbag that sat on the vanity. She fished out a bottle and her long fingernails clicked as she opened the lid and shook a white oval into her palm. "Take this pill to him. And don't be scared. Neil doesn't hold grudges."

Katie took the pill from the woman's hand. "But Neil's not crying anymore."

"Crying?"

"He told me these stop tears."

The woman snorted. "These stop pain, dear. That's the only time Neil cries. Wait until after me and Mr. Alcott have gone and then go find Neil. You won't be breaking any of AIDA's rules so don't worry."

Katie curled her fingers around the pill, grateful for any excuse to avoid Mr. Alcott. But as she nodded, he stepped into the bathroom and gave her a stern stare.

"Neil's correction mode is being controlled by AIDA. It's set at three and will stay at three until we return. If both of you have shown exceptionally good behavior, it will be turned down to a two. But I want to be very clear with you that neither AIDA nor myself will protect you from Neil. If I come home and find you strewn in pieces across the kitchen floor..." he finished his sentence with a shrug.

"Neil's not going to hurt you," Mrs. Alcott said quickly. "He wouldn't go through all that if he didn't want you here."

"AIDA has control over the refrigerator now," Mr. Alcott went on. "It will unlock for five minutes at noon so you can open it. Only take out one meal for each of you. If you touch it at any other time, it will shock you without the help of a chip."

"Yes sir," Katie said.

The man snapped his finger, and his wife took his arm. He sent her a final glare and towed the woman from the room. Katie sat, holding her breath until she heard the front door open and shut, followed by the mechanical grind of the lock.

She tiptoed down the hallway for the second time that day, finding the bathroom door wide and the couch abandoned. She cast a glance toward the door but continued to the kitchen to put water in a glass.

Her journey to the top of the stairs slowed with each step, but she forced herself onto the landing where the sailors continued their vigil on the side of the castle wall. She peeked into Neil's bedroom, frowning at the empty bed.

But as she turned away, she glimpsed a movement by the lion. Its snarl seemed to be directed toward her, but she forced herself to step inside the room anyway. Neil sat between the lion and the wall, stroking the animal's back. His eyes rose, his hands slowed, but didn't halt.

She approached slowly. "I'm sorry," she said.

His head jerked up, turning fearful eyes toward her. But, safe from AIDA's curse, she held out her offering.

He winced. Took the pill and glass, but only looked at them.

"Does the lion have a name?" she blurted.

He shook his head.

"Was it...alive when you got it?"

His eyebrows tucked, before he shook his head again. He snapped his hand to his mouth, swallowed the pill with a quick gulp and winced again.

"We should name him." Katie sat against the wall, pulling her knees to her chest. "Maybe that's why he looks so grumpy all the time."

His mouth twitched, though it was hard to tell if it was a grimace or a grin.

"Can I pet him too?"

Neil shrugged.

She suppressed a shudder and forced her fingertips across the long fur that circled the creature's head. Her fingers still tingled from AIDA's shock, and the fur added its own sensation, almost disguising the burn that lingered on her skin. There were many things she wanted to say, but she swallowed them.

Because now she knew that Neil wasn't the only one with ears in the room.

The World Within

WHAT IS A SHELL, EXCEPT the hollowed home of a creature now dead?
Crushed, extracted, eaten alive, or dissolved into an incessant batter of waves?
The exterior—dulled and rough—unnoticed, unseen; a shield of no value
until its pearlescent interior is ripped, exposed; the creature itself slashed and
torn.
A battle waged to hold itself together, a violent end, a valiant failure.
Now—and only now—the shell is transformed; the fallen shield rescued.
Its shimmering remains cherished, polished, placed on a shelf for all to see;
A coffin on display.

She had learned the poem in school, but she had forgotten it. Over the next few days, it had become a refrain in her head, like a song with no tune.

Her mind adapted to AIDA's rigid rules by numbing, but even after a week of exceptionally good behavior, AIDA remained at level four. Katie spent her days, gliding through a routine that only mimicked life and escaping into the recesses of her mind because it was the only place that AIDA could not breech.

She lay on the couch, next to Neil as he worked. He kept his eyes dutifully on the screen, while she gazed up at the ceiling, going through old memories like a half-forgotten dream.

"What is this, Dad?" Katie had asked, tracing the three holes that peered from the circle on the wall—a tiny face in a rectangle frame.

"That's an old plug," his father had answered.

She'd crawled onto her knees and closed one eye to peer into the slots. "What's it do?"

"It used to bring electricity into the house when your grandfather was little like you. It made things happen by themselves without anybody touching them."

"Like magic?"

"Sort of. Like lightning."

"Lightning is magic."

Her father laughed. "Sort of."

"Why don't we have lightning make things go by themselves now?"

"Well, they didn't use lightning. They used the sun. But taming nature is a dangerous business, Katie. Electricity belongs in the sky. Try to bring it to earth, and you're asking for trouble. Kind of like magic. What would you do if I gave you a wand you could wave and make anything you want to happen, anytime you wanted it to happen?"

"I'd heal your leg, so you don't limp no more."

Her father jolted, then smiled at her. "That's sweet. What else?"

"I'd wave it over the table and make breakfast show up. A big breakfast with pancakes and fruit and honey."

"And what else?"

"Mmm...I'd turn our walls purple."

"Purple?" Only in her memory did Katie pick up on the tinge of horror beneath the tone.

"Yeah, because you don't see purple very often. Only when the little flowers come out."

"What else?"

"I'd make the cotton grow so tall that it wouldn't hurt your back when you pick it."

"But then you couldn't pick it!"

"Well," Katie drawled. "Maybe I'd just wave the wand and it would pick itself. Like electricity."

"So, your wand would be doing all the cooking and cleaning and schoolwork for you?"

"No. I'd do my own schoolwork."

"What if everybody in the town had a wand and everything was happening by itself?"

Her mind had filled with silly images of people floating down the roads, bread bouncing onto counters, her teacher's chalk hovering over the board, her mother's shuttle darting between the strings of the loom like a water bug. She looked at her father and began to laugh.

"You're funny," she said, because it took too many words to say what she saw.

"That's what it was like when your grandpa was little. They didn't have wands, but they had lots of things that worked by themselves. They told the sun where to go, what to bring to life, and the sun did everything for them."

"Can we do that?"

"I imagine we could," her father replied. "But here's the thing. One day when your grandpa had just turned six years old, men made the sun stop coming through the plugs. Nobody knew why back then. It just stopped. Your grandpa's dad didn't know what to do. Most of the food had been kept cold by boxes that stole energy from the sun, and all that food went bad and smelly because nobody had salted it to keep it safe. People who weren't in their villages had to leave all their things and walk home. Lots of people died on the way or couldn't even find their villages because the sun machines had always told them where to turn.

"The sun's just like people. You can trap them and make them do your work for a while, but one day you're going to wake up and they're going to be gone, and you won't know how to do anything for yourself. It's a bad idea, Katie, enslaving the sun."

Katie shifted, glancing toward Neil as his keyboard ceased to clatter for just a few seconds. His eyes closed before he forced them open, pulled a leg close to the couch, and forced himself to start again.

"You're right, Dad," she thought. "It's a bad idea, enslaving the son."

The refrigerator, true to Mr. Alcott's words, only unlocked to let them pull out one meal at noon. Her stomach growled, but it would take a lot to break her down if Mr. Alcott planned on using food.

But not Neil, apparently. He huffed a frustrated breath, shakily typing the numbers that manipulated the lines on the screen, creating a fake world, adding a lime green color to the blades of pixel grass.

She studied the world he created. It was intriguing, but wrong. "Is it supposed to look real?"

He nodded.

"It doesn't," she answered.

His jaw tightened before he simultaneously swallowed and winced.

"Grass isn't that green, at least, not in my town. It's got more yellow than that."

He glanced toward her, his eyebrows tucking in thought, then typed a series of six numbers into the keyboard. The grass turned a sickly yellow green.

"Yeah, that looks more like home. Except our roads are mostly dirt and clumps of asphalt now. The roads broke up a long time ago."

Neil studied her, then typed a series of commands into the computer, creating first a brown line, then a wavy line, then a rocky texture, then nonuniform dark circles. Katie stared as the process slowly shaped, not home, not quite. But very close.

"Do you have to make the world look a certain way?" she asked.

He shrugged, then shook his head.

"Can you add a house—not like your house—a farmhouse?"

His eyebrows worked in thought before a white generic house showed up, something that didn't look like her home or his.

"It's made of wood," she said. "Most of the paint was white, but now it's peeling off."

His replica took longer to create, trying a few false attempts, but he eventually got the texture, then followed her request for windows and a porch.

"Yeah, that's close." Katie's eyes filled, and she turned them to the pages of her dictionary.

So many words, many no longer needed and others that may not be in the book. She glanced at AIDA, then flipped the pages with sudden inspiration. And there it was:

artificial intelligence

noun

1: a branch of computer science dealing with the simulation of intelligent behavior in computers

2: the capability of a machine to imitate intelligent human behavior

A machine. She flipped the page quickly before Neil could see, looking at the screen. Was AIDA connected with that? She'd seen computer carcasses before; after the Blackout, the elderly people in the village still talked about their parents pulling the machines apart to dig out the bits of gold in them, discarding them in a giant pile that had yet to break down. In school, they rearranged the old key caps to teach the little ones to read.

AIDA was a computer. She worked because she was hooked up to the electricity, which must be how she could access it to shock them. AIDA might not be so different from what was in Katie's grandfather's house before the Blackout. She swallowed, then flipped the page to the E section.

Electricity

noun

the time rate of flow of electric charge, in the direction that a positive moving charge would take and having magnitude equal to the quantity of charge per unit time: measured in amperes.

"Whatever that means," she muttered.

The curved lines on the front pages caught her eye as she began to close the book. She opened it again, smoothing out the page, feeling her heart slow as she again caught sight of Clark's handwriting.

She blinked before AIDA highlighted her tears. Wondering if Clark thought of her as much as she thought of him. Wondering what would have happened if she had stayed in her village.

"Neil," she asked. "Do you ever see people?"

He glanced at her, shut off his work, and flipped to another screen where a woman sat at a desk. She had blonde hair. Katie ground her teeth, thinking of the fabled brunettes that attended college with their luscious brown locks. This woman was older than college age, with fine lines around her eyes. She spoke straight to them, her voice tinged with a sense of urgency, dropping a few decibels like she was revealing a secret.

"Thirty-six people were killed this morning when a public transportation train ran off the rails. Authorities are investigating the driver, a thirty-six-year-old villager who was allowed to cross our borders from the outlying village of Findley's Wilderness. The deaths have sparked a heated debate among officials about this growing trend of issuing education and work visas to villagers. Meanwhile, in the north sector of town, a family was awakened when their AIDA alerted them of a man trying to gain access to their home..."

Neil let the woman talk for nearly an hour, the show flipping between the studio and bits of the outside world. Sometimes the buildings were lit by blue and red flashes. Sometimes victims were hidden beneath white cloths, carried by men in uniforms. Sometimes vehicles crashed into each other and rolled across the road.

Aware of Neil's eyes on her, Katie tried to cover any expressions. This was the city, the world outside of these four walls.

She clutched the dictionary to her chest like it would calm her heart. She swallowed hard.

Neil hit a button and brought his work back. "Lions...are...better," he said, measuring each word.

"My village isn't like yours," she said. "We have death, but most of the time people don't kill other people. And when anyone does, the entire village will hunt them down." Aware she was rambling, she glanced at him, but Neil had turned slightly toward her. "We don't have electricity," she said. "So, we can't fit more than a few people in a vehicle at a time. Most of the time we walk or ride a horse. Do you know what a horse is?"

He shook his head.

"It's...well, a little like a large gazelle, only without horns. My friend owns one. His name is Clark—the friend, not the horse. The horse's name is Midnight."

"Why did...you leave...your pride?" Neil asked suddenly.

"My pride?" Katie asked. "You mean...my village?"

He nodded.

It was an excellent question. "I guess I felt like there wasn't really a place for me there," she said. "My sister was getting married and Clark...well, things were going to change after school. And I guess I didn't want to stay, but I wish I had."

"Is Clark...your leader?"

"No, he's not our leader. But he is from the wealthy family. They own the well, so they control all the drinking water."

He nodded like it made perfect sense. "His pride."

"Yeah," she replied. "And his family doesn't want me in their pride."

He didn't reply right away, too busy swallowing from the effort of his first sentence. But he created a large pond on the screen, then said, "We are...a pride."

She said nothing, sat with trembling hands, biting the inside of her cheek, looking at the screen so she didn't have to look at him. "Two people don't make a pride, Neil."

"But..." Neil coughed, then shook his head.

Katie slid her feet to the floor, escaping to the kitchen to get him a drink. She clenched her teeth as she filled the glass, wondering what the Blackwells would think if they knew she could summon unlimited water with a turn of a handle while they were hoarding their bucketfuls. She carried the glass back, offering it to him. He took it, drank, managed to say one syllable, then shook his head in defeat.

"You know what's strange to think about?" Katie asked, eager to move away from the thought of prides. "You and I grew up only a few hours apart—at least in a truck. You can get water any time you want, but in my village even if we drill for it, it's very hard to find a spring. So where does your water come from?"

"River?"

"I doubt it," she said. "Our river water can make people very sick, and it flows from here so yours probably isn't much better." She pulled her knees to her chest and hugged her legs. "That's what killed my parents. When I was ten, it didn't rain for months. All of the cotton died, and we drank all the rainwater we had stored. So Dad sold some of our chickens and bought a jug of water from the Blackwells. He let us girls drink one glass from the jug every morning and evening, but he boiled the water from the river for himself and Mom. That usually worked. But this time it didn't. Mallory found them the next morning. She screamed so much she couldn't talk for two days. And you know the worst part? It rained the day we buried them."

Neil frowned as she spoke, but he only asked, "What is rain?"

"In my village, sometimes water falls from the sky. In drops, one at a time. Sometimes just a few. We call that 'sprinkling' but sometimes it comes in a downpour like a giant shower. That's called rain. Sometimes so much water stays on the ground that you can kick it up. When it rains, we put out every pot and pan we have in the house and collect as much water as we can. Even if it rains while we're at school, some of us will run home if no one at the house is around to collect the water."

"How do...you spell?" Neil asked, pulling her from her thoughts.

"What?"

"Rain."

"R-a-i-n," she answered.

Neil typed, pulling up a list of numbers. He inserted a string between the lines of numbers and suddenly his landscape was marked by falling white lines.

He smiled. "That?"

Katie looked up. Swallowed.

"No. Not that, Neil. That is rain, but it's not real. You can't feel it on your skin, it doesn't make your hair wet and run off your chin. The real world isn't on a screen. It can't be made on a screen."

Neil's eyes slit. He punched a button and the rain disappeared. His fingers jabbed the buttons, causing mountains to appear in the background, adding mist to float around them.

"This...is our world," he said. "All we get."

The Choice

SHE WOKE, FACING THE holes Neil had punched in her wall. She shoved back the covers, almost dramatically, to reinforce to AIDA and any Alcott parent that may be watching that she was not sleeping late. Gathered her dress, wondering if it had been chosen for Neil's pleasure just like she had. Walked to the bathroom. Relaxed only after the door was locked and AIDA could no longer see her.

"Hot," she said. The water in the shower responded with a torrential rain and within thirty seconds, the steam began to coat the glass.

She waited in front of the mirror over the sink until their messages appeared.

Am I allowed to leave?

NO.

Are YOU allowed to leave?

NO. I TOLD THEM NOT TO BRING YOU.

She gripped the sink, feeling guilt and anger alternate in sweeping waves and watching her eyes change from a dull, tear-rimmed gaze into a red glint as tiny blood vessels buckled beneath the pressure. She gripped the edges of the bathroom counter, felt her jaw tighten, heard the refrain in her head.

This is our world. All we get.

She no longer fought her anger, for anger was sadness transformed. Sadness only crippled. Anger...

She stomped to the doorway, rolled her tight shoulders into performance mode, and smoothed the lines of the skin around her eyes from their tiny stripes of betrayal. She walked on borrowed time, but each day was another step she must take. Follow every rule, appease every hurt, perform every task, stifle every heart cry.

For now.

She closed her eyes. She couldn't keep on like this. She steeled herself with a breath and pushed open the door, already analyzing where AIDA was and what her face needed to show as she walked down the hallway.

Neil had one lamp on the side table. She turned on the second and sat down. He glanced over at her, his fingers never slowing. Offered a small smile, a curious glance.

She swallowed, pulling her knees up while she pushed the thought away. "Last night I dreamed that everything you created on that screen became real. You put a door into one of these walls, and I thought it went outside. But when I ran through it, you were in a room with about twenty lions, just hanging out. And I stopped and stared at you and said, 'you would.'"

Neil's smile grew until he barked a laugh that lasted three seconds before his body jolted. He yelped, but the sound only set AIDA off again. Neil grabbed the pillow, pressed his entire face into it to muffle the second cry.

"AIDA, stop!" Katie called. "Deactivate!"

"I'm sorry," AIDA replied. "I am not synced with your voice."

Neil lowered the pillow, rubbing his eyes.

"Why'd she shock you for laughing?" Katie demanded.

"Loud," Neil said. He blinked back tears as he turned to retrieve the keyboard.

"Sorry," Katie said.

The word made Neil brace, but nothing happened.

Katie uncurled herself from the couch, moving to the upstairs bathroom where Mrs. Alcott had left the little pills. She struggled to pop the lid off, hoping that electricity never made a comeback to her village, that the Blackout had thoroughly fried the wires and buttons so they would never work again. Wondered what it was that made the electricity stop coming through the wires in the first place.

She lifted her eyes to the five small globes that lit Mrs. Alcott's mirror, wondering how much electricity would be needed before the breakers were flipped and AIDA blacked out. Had Neil ever tried to use it up? There was no way to ask him. No way to get his consent for an experiment that could backfire so badly. But if AIDA lost her power, she could no longer control the door or report if someone went through it.

Katie paused.

She popped the lid back onto the bottle, replaced it into the cabinet, cupping the pill in her hand. She walked out of the bathroom, leaving the light on. AIDA said nothing as she went to her room to pick up the dictionary she didn't actually need.

She pretended to drop the pill and clapped at the lamps next to the bed. They turned on and, with the pill safely in her hand, she crawled to investigate the carpet. Feigning finding the pill, she rose, again conveniently forgetting to clap out the lamps. Still, AIDA said nothing.

Her heart sped as she walked down the stairs, making her way to the kitchen to get a glass of water. Another flip of a switch flooded the room with light. She fished the coffee pot from its place, poured in water, and hit the brew button. Still AIDA gave no response, but Katie imagined the machine huddled in a dark corner, trembling because she realized her time was short.

She plugged in the toaster and fished two slices of bread from the basket, aware that she was on the radar now that she was near the food. But two slices were allowed, and she pushed them into the toaster, then turned it to the darkest setting she thought she could get away with. There was nothing else she could do in the kitchen with the food locked in the refrigerator, so she padded back to the living room, hitting the switch to the overhead lights and turning on the fan.

"You don't mind, do you?" she asked, then offered the pill and glass to Neil.

He took it, gave her a flicker of a smile, then swallowed the pill without the help of the water.

The coffee began to gurgle, promising fuel that would get them through the morning until the refrigerator unlocked. She sat on the couch for ten minutes, but the lights stayed on and strong. She glanced toward Neil, wondering how to communicate her plans, but there was so little she could say. If he understood what she meant, his father could too.

"Do you think your mom would mind if I lit one of the candles?" she asked, then offered a playful smile. "It's more romantic that way, don't you think?"

He glanced over, surprised, confused.

She swallowed, already feeling stupid with the role. "Do you know what romantic means?"

He shook his head slowly.

"Oh." Well good. "Do you think your mom would mind if I let the candle?"

Again, he shook his head.

She stood. She felt her fists clench and forced them to relax. She *had* to speak this way if his parents were going to hear. She pulled open drawers, then seized the match box and slid it into her pocket. She lit one of the scented candles, letting it burn obscurely on the table. What if they guessed? What if she couldn't use up enough electricity to black out AIDA? She was running out of electronics.

The refrigerator beeped. Neil threw aside the keyboard, but she beat him to the kitchen door. She lurched to open the refrigerator, reaching for the top two boxes while trying to count the remaining. Only six boxes left. Three days until they would run out again. Would Neil's parents return then? Would the man drop groceries through the door, unaware that he was the sole lifeline for two captives?

One. One captive.

Neil had never even tried to run. He belonged in this world.

She pulled two containers from the boxes, swallowing at the meager portions. Wondering if Neil was beginning to rethink his choice to keep her and endure a slow starvation subsiding on one meal a day.

The house was filled with buzzing, like tiny insects humming away, sending a steady trickle of sunlight to each appliance, but denying the smallest ray to her and Neil. The coffee sputtered as it reached the end of its water supply. She opened the door to the microwave and slid the frozen meal inside. Sent up a silent prayer.

She hit start. The tiny light bulb flipped on, illuminated the tray that began to pivot. Then a brilliant pop of light. She heard a shatter, saw a tiny shard of glass illuminated in flight before it plunged into darkness as deep as any overcast night in the woods.

Neil yelped from the living room. Katie stood, her heart battering her chest.

"AIDA," Neil rasped. "Reactivate."

The darkness embraced her, challenged only by the tiny candle that flickered in the corner.

"AID—," Neil tried louder, his word ending in a choke.

Her hands trembled. Why was he calling back the thing with the power to hurt him? The ability to relock that door?

She abandoned the candle, slipping behind the counter and crawling along it as Neil crashed into something in the living room. Even in the wilderness, she'd never moved through such complete darkness. On her hands and knees, she inched her way across the floor, waving her hand before her to find her way.

"Katie?" Neil called.

Katie crawled on. Her hand hit stone. She pivoted into the entryway.

"AIDA! Activate!" Desperation wobbled Neil's voice.

She swallowed, feeling her chest burn. But he wanted her in his pride. He'd never voiced any desire to leave. He wouldn't let her leave either.

"Katie? Okay?"

Her fingertips brushed the wall as she crawled toward the door. A crack of light showed beneath the lip, beckoning. She reached for the light, found the door, ghosted her fingers toward the handle. She put one foot beneath her, straightened slowly. One pull and daylight would betray her.

"Katie! Alive?"

The candle in the kitchen sent erratic light as Neil lifted it.

Katie yanked against the door.

It yielded a fourth of an inch. Then metal hit metal, its journey stopped short, sending vibrations down her spine.

"No," she breathed.

She yanked again. The dead bolt held fast.

"No!" She kicked the delivery door. "No, no, no! Out!"

Behind her, the candle floated through the darkness, then made a sudden dart to the side where it settled into a steady hover.

Neil's arms wrapped around her chest, pinning her arms, pulling her back into the void.

She flailed, trying to kick him.

He sat on the tile, wrapping one leg over hers, pinning them against his opposite shin.

"Calm," he said, repeating with a more distressed tone, "Calm. I'll...protect you."

"I don't want protection, I want out!"

"Candle, see?" Neil said. "AIDA will...come back. Storm...maybe."

She swallowed her screams, trying to find logic again. He thought a storm halted the electricity. Would his parents? No. No, there would be a fine. Mr.

Alcott hated fines. She closed her eyes, pretending that was the only reason it was dark.

"Calm. We'll get...more light." He coughed.

There were two more candles in the house, one in the bedroom upstairs, one in the bathroom. She'd counted them all. She breathed deeper and deeper, forcing herself to calm down when she only wanted to run.

His arms loosened.

"No," she said. "Don't light the others. They'll burn down too quickly, and we'll be left in the dark."

"AIDA...will come again."

She shivered, crawled closer to the candle that now outlined the side table where Neil had set it. "It's not a storm, Neil," she said. "I killed AIDA."

The silence that followed was unusual, even for the man who rarely spoke.

She felt his eyes swing to her. She pulled her knees to her chest, hugging them. "I thought it would unlock the door. And now we're stuck."

"You...killed AIDA?"

"She's not responding, is she? He's going to know. You have to help me get out."

"Don't leave." The same level of panic crept into his voice.

"You can come too!"

"No. No, I'll..." He stopped panting long enough to swallow. "I'll protect you. Promise."

"If you want to protect me, help me get the door open!"

"AIDA..."

"AIDA's dead!"

Several seconds stretched. All she heard was his strained breath.

"I'm sorry," he said.

"Neil, please..." Katie trailed off.

Two seconds passed. Five. Ten.

"I'm sorry," Neil said again.

The air was still, so still she felt the puff of his breath as he began to laugh.

"See?" she whispered. "See, she can't control you anymore. We can break down the door. We can get out of here before your father comes back."

Neil's laugh stopped, followed shortly by his breath. She felt him lean back before he suddenly rose.

"No," he said.

"What?"

He moved away from her, lifted the candle above her head. It lit his face, distorting his features but illuminating a very real glare. He swallowed, once, twice. But his lips never even opened to try and speak. His eyes flashed with rage. He turned, found his way up the stairs, and took the candle with him.

The Confession

A PAIR OF SCISSORS was no match for one inch of steel. Katie sawed in the dark, feeling the teeth of her blade file smoother with each pass. She sawed, driven by the idea that one steel bolt was all that kept her from freedom. She sawed because every second brought Mr. Alcott and his wrath closer to the door. She sawed because it was pitch black, because even finding her way to the kitchen drawer and back had been a challenge. She sawed because she had no idea what else to do.

The door was installed backward, its hinges hidden on the outside. It was steel, not wood, so it wouldn't splinter or burn. She jammed the knife into the crack again, pulled hard. A sliver of sunlight appeared. Then the blade snapped, pinched between the lip.

She fell back, sitting in the darkness. Her tears felt warm, sliding fast, leaving a sticky trail behind. The air was growing hot and stale.

She had made mistakes in her life, but most of them could be patched with an apology and an atonement or, at the least, interference from a third party who had stepped in to soften the blow. This one couldn't be fixed.

She couldn't turn back the clock. She'd gambled and she'd lost. Clark would never know how hard she'd tried to return to him. Mallory would assume she'd embraced city life and left them all behind without a second thought. Tucker would wait every second Saturday in vain. And she…she wasn't sure what would happen to her. If Mr. Alcott would kill her, if he'd punish her first, or if he'd drag her off to sell as a proper slave.

Terror returned, and her imagination fled her body, crashing around the layout of the house, searching for any object that could set her free.

It came up with nothing. Her chest tightened; the tears created a stream.

She hadn't wanted this, hadn't signed up to be shut away in a house with a man who built entire worlds, but didn't know how to function like a normal human in his own.

And she couldn't stop it. AIDA was broken. The electricity wouldn't come back until someone fixed it, until the fine was paid, and that wouldn't happen until Mr. Alcott returned.

Unless the man who could fix AIDA came first.

Hope flickered. She crawled to the end of the entryway, flailing one arm in the darkness before her. Neil had the candle; if she found the light, she would find him.

She patted her way to the stairs, counted them as she climbed until her hand hit carpet instead of another ledge.

The air was a fuzzy gray now, not black, and a dim glow came from Neil's bedroom. She crawled to the door, peering toward the tiny flame on the nightstand.

He sat on the floor next to the lion with his face pressed against his knees. His arm lay across his shins, limp, fingers loosely holding items she couldn't make out.

She could have found him even in the dark, for his breaths were long, loud, and strained.

"Neil," she whispered, then scooted closer. "I had a thought. If the repair man came, or whoever gives the fine, would they knock on that door? Because if they did, we could shout through it. Or could you pay the fine, and then when the electricity comes back on, we could try to jam the door when the delivery man comes? Or–"

His fingers tightened. He lifted his head, but his eyes were gloomy. He swallowed. Opened his mouth, took a breath to speak, then let it out.

Katie sat, pulling her knees against her chest, watching his eyes rove with the effort of choosing which words would convey the most meaning with the least effort. She waited so long, she almost guessed he wouldn't talk at all.

But then he asked, "Why do you...hate me?"

"What?" Katie blinked. "I don't, Neil."

"I called. You sneaked. Left me...to be hurt."

Her body froze. Shame washed in, but it came with a second wave of anger.

"He wouldn't have hurt you, Neil, not if *I* had escaped. That's why I didn't tell you, so you had nothing to do with it. And for that matter, why did you let them bring me? You told them not to, so you knew they were going to lock me up the moment I walked in, and you said nothing! Nothing!" She dropped her voice; the tears made it shake but the words still poured out in a sob. "You deserve everything he does to you."

His eyes hardened. His chest heaved, like a dying wave, each breath growing tighter until he stopped altogether.

Katie swallowed, regretting her words, but she'd put them out and now she had to stand behind them. She saw pain flash through his face before it went blank. She dropped her own eyes, adding, "Besides, he's gonna punish me, not you. And I probably deserve it."

Then, from the nightstand, came the shrill call of the phone. They both jumped.

"How? I thought AIDA..." Katie sputtered.

"Landline," Neil rasped, then rolled sideways to answer. He flailed in the dark, waving his hand, whimpered at the second ring, and nearly panted at the third as his hand made contact. He snatched the receiver and dutifully rasped, "Yes?"

Mr. Alcott's voice made Katie's heart sting, so loud that his words were distinct this time. "Neil! Is Katie still there?"

"Yes. Dark."

"Didn't you warn her about the electricity?"

"Honey, we all forgot," Mrs. Alcott's voice echoed through, small and distant. "We forgot, too, you and me. She didn't know, she didn't mean to, did she, sweetheart? It was just a mistake, wasn't it, Neil?"

Neil's eyes lifted to hers, but she never saw them meet because she'd already squeezed hers shut. She heard him swallow.

"Forgot," Neil said. His voice grew steady, repeating, "I forgot."

Katie's body shook in a burst of silent sobs that grew as Mr. Alcott took a deep breath.

"I will pay the fine," the man said. "I will ask them to turn the electricity back on, but I don't expect they'll bother coming until Monday and by then you are going to be three days behind in your work, so you're going to have to catch up or we're going to be fined for that too. You do whatever it takes to make sure Katie never does this again."

"Yes," Neil said, his voice breathy, almost hopeful.

Katie ventured a peek, finding him still searching for her eyes, questioning if she could hear it.

She wouldn't be taken. She wouldn't be killed. His lie had saved her.

"And Neil," Mr. Alcott said. "When AIDA comes back on, it's going up to an eight."

Neil's face drained all color. His pupils, already larger in the candlelight expanded so much they nearly hid all traces of hazel. His lips opened like he would pant if he had any breath. The voice that came sounded very different from the one Katie knew. It was higher and smaller and scared.

"Dad..."

"Do not call me that!" Mr. Alcott roared. "You are grown like a man; you are punished like a man! It goes to an eight and if you do as you are told, you will only feel it once."

"But that's..." Katie began.

Neil pressed his fingers against her mouth. They were cold. They shook. But he rasped. "Yes."

"I will try to get the lights back on as soon as I can," Mr. Alcott repeated. "Your mother and I will be back on Monday. Until then, you and Katie will have to make do."

"Yes," Neil's voice cracked.

Mrs. Alcott spoke quickly, "There are candles in the..."

Her voice cut off. The silence settled.

The candle burned between them.

Neil hung up without looking.

"Neil..." Katie began but after that there wasn't much to say.

She bit her tongue against anything involving the word 'sorry' and instead whispered, "Help me get out. I want to go home. And...if you do...you can come too."

The darkness thickened.

"To your home?"

"My village, yes."

She heard his fingernail run across the material, once, twice, three times.

"Are there lions?"

"No," she answered. "I've never seen a lion except on your screen. So maybe that means the other things on the screen aren't really outside either."

His huff bordered on disappointment. "I want...lions."

"But if we get the door open," she said, "you can be free too. Your dad can't hurt you anymore, and you can see the rain for real."

"And...we live there?"

"Yeah. You can meet my sister and my...friends."

"Will they...hurt?"

"No. It's not like a lion pride. Everyone shares the land—or they have their own parts of it. We just have to force the door open."

"Before they return."

"Yeah," she said. "Before your dad can turn it onto an eight."

"If...he knows...we tried...he'll take you," Neil rasped.

"Probably."

"He...will. Like...the other."

She searched the darkness between them. "What other?"

"He took her."

"How long was she here?"

"Two days."

"Where did he take her?"

"Away."

"And then?"

"Don't know."

She couldn't speak. Her throat closed as though each second was pulling a noose tighter.

"Could stay," Neil said. "No trouble."

She watched the candle flicker, as though it was running out of fuel. She imagined the years ahead, filled with food that didn't have to be cooked, a house regulated by cool air from the vents, unlimited water so abundant she could swim in it if she knew how. Neil would keep plodding forward like a faithful workhorse. They could have every luxury she could ever want if they were willing to do everything they were told exactly the way they were told to do it.

She thought of her village. The harvests in the heat of summer, huddling next to the fire in the winters, the hunger that came every spring, the snide looks from the family that ruled the town.

But also Mallory's chatter as she made homemade biscuits that practically melted beneath the white gravy. The dances that came after the workday was over. The surge of excitement seeing Tucker's truck rattle up the road with its treasures, watching the cotton bloom and look like pictures they'd seen of snow.

Life in the village was unpredictable, filled with emotional highs and lows, friends and enemies, and problems that needed to be fixed before they grew worse. It was...life.

She looked at the dead lion, the closest thing Neil ever had for a companion, with the exception of two days with a girl who'd probably been just as panicked as Katie felt.

She swallowed. "We have to try, Neil. I can't explain life in the village to you. It's hard in a different way than here, but it's worth it. We could have whole different lives. But you have to help me. I can't do it by myself."

Neil took a breath, then answered, "Yes."

The Promise

THE DOOR HAD HELD FAST between each of Neil's blows, but the frame of the delivery door trembled after each strike, its screws wiggling in their holes. They'd scoured the house, but the best tool they'd come up with was an old bowling ball stuffed away in Mr. Alcott's closet. They'd wrapped it in a pillowcase.

Now, here she was, watching Neil gasp with breath that only grew heavier as the metal bowed, the corners of the frame loosening and beginning to pull apart. His movements had begun with precision, but gradually landed on either side of his aim as he tired. But a burst of fear lent him both speed and power. Katie stepped back as the man took out years of rage on the delivery door that brought him a taste of the world but refused to let him step into it.

The steel shattered at the corners, the deformed square finally bowing before the man. Neil gasped for breath, heaved the ball, and knocked the movable shelf free. Moonlight glowed through the gap in the door.

"Neil, you did it," Katie whispered.

The man began to pant. "I don't want...you gone."

"We have to," she said. "We have to go. Together, remember?" She dropped to her knees and tucked her head into the square, twisting to fit her shoulders and grunting as she slithered, squeezing her ribs, scraping her stomach against the broken levers of the mechanical shelf. Even Allison would struggle to fit through this hole. There was no way Neil could leave unless the door was opened from the outside.

Crisp, cooler air hit her face. Her eyes ached as she stood and surveyed the horizon where dim yellow lights twinkled from the rectangles of every window, as though the rooms sought to outshine the stars.

House after house blocked her view, the lines of rooftops broken only by the scraggly branches of an occasional tree. Her muscles tensed as she crouched, resisting the urge to flee with the instinct of a wild animal.

"Katie?" The door muffled Neil's voice. "Me too?"

She turned back toward the narrow square opening. Her hand hovered over the numbered buttons above the handle.

"Neil, there's a code!" she called.

"Three, nine, six, four, nine, eight," Neil called softly.

Katie punched in the numbers, growling when they didn't light.

"Neil, there's no electricity!"

"Don't leave me!" Neil's voice rose closer to a shout than she'd ever heard.

"I'm not, just..." She took a breath and pressed her thumb against the latch. The hateful bolt obeyed with a simple click. She pushed the door inward. The hallway was so dark, it seemed to suck in the starlight.

Neil stepped across the threshold, wrapping his arms around her in a crushing hug. Her face was against his chest, but she hugged him back. "You really thought I was going to leave you?"

"You're everything, Katie," he said. "All I have."

Her heart sank, but it was Neil who let go. He blinked at the red streetlights that guarded the sidewalks. His face pivoted to one side, then the other, blinking rapidly as his gaze followed the stretching sidewalks. His face lifted toward the stars, with eyes so wide she could see pinpoints of reflection into them.

"They're watching," he whispered.

"What?" She followed his stare toward the lights in the sky. "No, those are stars. That's...natural electricity. It's a ball of swirling light. There's no AIDA up there."

His eyes lowered slowly toward hers, then rose again. "Not true."

"Those are stars. They've been there forever."

Neil cast a glance back toward the safety of the house before he said, "Must run."

They jogged across the driveway, turning the corner, fleeing to the backyard where the houses created squares of shadows. Katie stalled, searching the low moon, useless now when she had no idea whether it was setting or rising.

Houses behind her. Houses in front of her. She searched for a distant tree line. Trees grew near rivers. Home was upstream. Find the river. Find home.

But all she saw were buildings. She closed her eyes trying to remember her arrival. She'd been huddled on the right side of the car, and she'd stepped out near the sidewalk to the door. Had they turned in from the right or left?

Right. They'd turned from the right. She remembered that she'd used her feet to press against the door. "Follow me. The market was that way. Somewhere."

Neil stood, roving the horizon with glazed eyes.

"Neil! We have to walk."

He glanced at her. "Never—been out."

"I know," she whispered, mostly to herself. She released a slow breath, then extended her hand. "Come on. Hold my hand."

His eyes lifted toward her, wary. "It's big," he said. "Too big."

"It's okay. I know the way," she said. "We have to go. Before your dad gets back. They'll fine him, remember? He hates fines. And then he's going up to an eight."

Neil's face grayed. His eyes lowered. He nodded. Grabbed her hand.

She swallowed, then led him down the sidewalk. The farther they got from the house, the more she relaxed and the harder he gripped. The uneven ground taunted her heels, threatening the thin soles of the shoes his mother had purchased for her...or for the girl before her.

"What was her name?" she asked.

"Who?"

"The other girl."

He shrugged.

"You don't know?"

"Never said. Just screamed."

Katie swallowed. "Is that why you kept holding my mouth until I promised not to scream?"

Neil nodded. "She screamed. He took her."

"Where'd your parents get her?"

"Market."

Katie walked faster. The market sold girls. But it was the only way she knew to get home. Still, Tucker had said she was safe with her sponsors. At least, she would have been if they hadn't been bent on bringing her home for their captive son's bride.

As the sky lit into a gray haze, the houses grew fewer and the trees grew taller. Lights began to outline windows as people woke, and headlights swept the yards whenever an occasional car pulled out of a driveway.

Katie set her eyes on the trees, tugging Neil as he spun this way, then that, sometimes even trying to walk backward.

"Neil, stop," she whispered. "Walk straight ahead and only look with your eyes. It's just like your screen world, okay? You can look better when we get out of the town."

Neil obediently fell into step next to her, but he lifted his head to look at the sky. The sun was beginning to lighten the undersides of several thin clouds with a pale pinkish hue. "It's not screen world. It goes up."

"Have you really never been outside?" Katie stopped to stare at him.

Neil shook his head.

"Not ever. Not even for a moment?"

He squirmed then shook his head again. "No memory."

"Why?"

"It's not safe."

"It's safe for your parents. Why not you?"

Neil blinked. "Don't know."

"Do you get paid for your work?"

Neil shook his head.

"So what?" Katie snapped. "They just locked you inside and left you doing unpaid work all day while they fly around the country for conferences? You're a grown man, why would you put up with that?"

"AIDA tells," Neil said. "No trouble, no shocks. Nowhere to go."

"Your mom said your dad didn't shock you very often."

Neil huffed a laugh and raised his eyebrows. "Mom lies."

Katie's heart tugged and for a moment she let herself really look at the man. Her eyes pricked. She stepped forward, hugging his chest. He stiffened but after a minute his arms closed around her shoulders.

"I'm sorry I tried to leave you," Katie said. "I thought you would stop me from going."

"AIDA stops," Neil said. "Not me."

"AIDA is dead now." Katie pulled back, squeezing his hand. "She doesn't get to control either of us anymore."

Neil lifted his eyes to stare far past the houses around them, past the doors that could open and expose them if the wrong person stood on the threshold. They fixated at the end of the road where the sun broke through.

"Katie," he whispered. "The sky is pink."

"Yes it is," she answered.

"Not...blue?"

"Oh." Katie glanced back toward the painted colors. "It will be blue. That's the sunrise. It's always pink, purple, and orange first."

Neil huffed a laugh. "Sun...doesn't rise."

"What?" Katie answered.

Neil dropped her hand to show a stationary finger. "Sun stays still. Earth moves." He circled one finger around the other. "Earth rises."

She knew that from the science books, though she'd often wondered if it was an error. But his attention had been at least temporarily arrested by the display of a world he'd only seen on a screen, a display that kept him walking in the right direction.

"It does?" she asked and tugged him into a walk. "How does that work?"

They traveled another ten steps before he shook his head and replied, "Too many words."

Katie frowned as they came upon an intersecting road and the buildings began to look a little like shops. The market must be on the opposite side of the city.

Behind her, Neil's footsteps stopped again.

Katie spun, resisting a growl.

He blinked from behind splayed fingers.

"Neil?"

"Hurts," he wailed.

She lifted her own eyes to the expansive pale blue, the golden beams showering the land. "The dawn?"

"Why's it...so bright?"

"It's not. Not yet." She reached for his hand. "Close your eyes if you have to. Just follow me."

He whimpered. Lowered his fingers to catch her hand. She gave him a reassuring smile. Felt his fingers tighten. She took a step, came to the end of her arm, and jerked against it like a tethered boat.

"Neil, come on. I'll lead you."

Neil swallowed. "Go back."

"We can't go back, remember? AIDA's there."

"AIDA's dead."

"Your parents are there, and they'll bring AIDA back," she said. "We have to find my village—my pride—remember?"

He grimaced. "Prides don't like...outside lions."

"We're not lions, Neil," she said. "They'll like you. I promise."

Her heartbeat was turning into a war drum as he delayed their escape.

Neil studied her, then glanced at the streets around them. "Stay here."

"We can't stay here," she said. "We'd get caught; we couldn't survive here. We need other people to survive. My kind of people."

"I don't have...others."

"Your parents took care of you. They brought you everything you needed."

"Yes."

Katie stared at the man. Tucker had warned her against going to the market on her own, and she still had to get past the checkpoint. She'd never make it out of the city without Neil.

"Well," she fumbled, "your parents must have had some reason to hide you when you were a kid from the town. But the city people don't normally come to my village. So you'd be safe there. We don't have AIDAs, so no one can shock you. You could be free."

He swayed toward her. His eyes glittered like a starved animal.

"Please, Neil," she said. "Come with me. Just try it. If you don't like it, you can come back to the city."

His fingers gripped tighter. "And you come?"

She caught the refusal before it left her lips.

He stood, rooted like a tree.

She kept her eyes on the weave of his shirt. Tasted the lie, felt its bitterness on her tongue. "Yes."

His chest expanded as he drew in a slow breath. His grip lessened, palm cradling hers, though his fingers trembled. "How..." He trailed off, searching for a word. "How many steps?"

"How far? I don't know," she answered. "It might take a few days, or we could find them by tonight. I came in the truck. I don't know how long it will take to walk up the river."

He frowned. "That killed your father."

"Yes."

She began to walk so quickly, she nearly panted. The sun warmed the air around them, its rays penetrating her skin. It felt so good, but she glanced toward Neil's arm, frowning at its paleness. If he'd truly never been out of the house, he'd burn by noon.

But they couldn't stop. Not in the city. If she could get out of the inborder by noon, they could find the woods and walk in the shade. And if there wasn't enough shade, they could find somewhere and sleep. Traveling at night might be safer anyway.

Neil stumbled, almost breaking her hand as he caught his balance.

She glanced toward his squinting eyes, slowing her pace. "I'm sorry."

How was he going to manage life in her village? If he couldn't handle sunlight, how was he going to hold up when the temperature rose to the hundreds or fell to the twenties? Jeremy and Mallory didn't have a room for him unless she shared hers. And what would he do when he found out about Clark?

But what was her choice? He didn't have any money; he couldn't live in the city on his own. At least in the village, he could find a job, maybe live with the family he worked for, fall in love with someone else, and get a little place of his own.

She swallowed. "Things will get easier when we find my village."

Neil frowned. "Your pride...didn't want you."

She wet her lips. "I think I didn't want them."

"I want you."

"I know you do," she said.

Even the smallest of smiles summoned his.

"So we stay here," he said. "Together."

Her heart sank.

"I can't stay here, Neil. But I promise you that my people will want you. But I can't get to them without you."

Neil's smile slipped. He blinked twice and she panicked, seeing his thoughts begin to stir. She grabbed his hands. "If you get us there..."

She stalled as her mind screamed not to make promises. But she'd already spoken. He was waiting, watching her intently, hopefully. "We can...start new lives," she stammered.

He blinked, his eyebrows quivering with confusion. "But...together, yes?"

Regret flowered into full bloom. Her throat closed so tightly she nearly choked on her breath. "If...if you want," she managed.

Her breath closed completely, but he let out his in a relieved sigh. "It's all I want," he said. "To not...be alone."

"You won't be alone," Katie said. "There's a lot of people in our village."

"But only one Katie."

"Yeah." She huffed a miserable laugh. "Only one Katie."

The Road Home

A LOW HUM ROSE FROM behind as a car slowed, then blinded them with a flash of blue and red lights. Neil grunted, turning his face away, squeezing his eyes shut, yet he still managed to clutch her hand. Katie took a step to run, but Neil rooted both of them.

She swallowed, swaying back toward him. It wasn't against a law to walk down the road, was it? Had AIDA somehow tattled on them?

Neil forced his eyes to fully open and pulled in a deep breath as a man in a tailored gray uniform stepped out of the car. The officer smiled at them. "Hello there!"

Katie opened her mouth, but Neil squeezed her hand before he replied, "Hello."

"One of the neighbors called," the man said. "They didn't recognize you. Are you visiting someone in this neighborhood?"

Neil pulled in a deep breath before he spoke, "We are going to the market." Neil kept his voice from cracking, but his tone sounded like it was scraping lightly against his chords.

"Oh?" The officer stepped closer, his eyes flickering down Katie's body. "I can save you the trouble. How much you want for her?"

Katie fought to keep her breath under control, but now it was her fingers tightening around Neil's.

He took another breath, let it out. Then sucked in another and said the most words she'd ever heard him manage. "We're going to buy. Not sell. She is to carry...the things home."

The officer frowned, shifting his weight toward Neil. "Show your ID."

Katie resisted a look at the car to see if the door was unlocked because she could hear it running, but a second officer sat in the passenger seat watching her.

She couldn't say anything, not without breaking Neil's charade that she was his slave. And was it even a charade? He could sell her to this man right now; they could load her into that car and take her wherever they wanted. Nobody would ever know.

Neil held out his hand, palm up, like he was attempting what he thought was a shake, but the officer passed a black box over his wrist.

A voice like AIDA's, only a male version, came from the box. "Neil Alcott. Simulator landscape programmer. Address: Number three on street B. Citizenship Class A. No restrictions."

The officer's knees had stiffened at the announcement of Neil's citizenship class, but he took a step back after the announcement was completed. "You mentioned you got turned around. Would you like an escort to the market?"

Neil shook his head, then replied, "Only directions. It's a nice day to walk." He'd kept himself from croaking, but his voice was rapidly moving to a strained higher pitch. Katie peeked at him.

His face remained emotionless, but he was in pain; his eyes were beginning to shine with moisture.

But there was no need for him to continue to speak. The officer swung his arm to point further down the street, giving a series of right and left turns and numbers of blocks. Katie tried to remember the pattern but ended up with a mental image of a squiggly line of questionable lengths.

Neil at least sounded confident as he said, "Thank you."

"My pleasure," said the officer. Then he climbed back into the car, pulled onto the road to make a large turn, and glided out of the neighborhood.

"Who *are* you?" Katie asked.

Neil panted twice, wiped a full tear out of his eye. He took a breath and looked down at her. "Neil Alcott."

"Who are the Alcotts?"

"Class A," Neil said. "Dad...secures political prisons." His eyes flickered down. "No one escapes."

His words scared even himself, and he towed her quickly down one street, then a turn, another two blocks, another turn. She said nothing, afraid to break his concentration, unsure if his turns were right or wrong, but he had as good a chance at being right as she did.

The market. She had lost track of days, wasn't sure when Tucker would be there. But even if he wasn't, the road home was just beyond it. The road ran by the river in some places. If they could find the road, they could find the river. If they could find the river, they could follow it home.

The houses changed into higher buildings, like workshops but completely enclosed, and it was impossible to tell what the merchant sold from outside. The city was noisy, mostly covering the occasional birds with cars, honking, and people talking to devices strapped on their wrists as they walked past. No cars crashed into each other; no bodies were brought out covered with sheets. Neil's city was larger than her village, louder and busier, but still different from what had been portrayed on the screen when he had let her watch the humans.

They walked on, collecting curious glances but no one else spoke to them. The buildings began to shrink and become spaced out. Houses reappeared. And still Neil walked on, making each turn without hesitation. Until he stopped, lifting his head to survey the fence of metal ahead, the links offering a glimpse of the expanse at the other side, blocked only by signs that read: Electrical Fence. Do not touch.

Neil read it the moment she did, and it elicited the first noise from his mouth in half an hour: a whimper. A long line of trucks stretched back from a gate and beside it a guard stood at a small entryway where people showed their wrists before passing through.

"You have no restrictions in town," she said quickly. "They'll let you through."

Neil sighed, looking at her, his eyes already dulling with defeat. "Maybe not you."

Katie chewed her lip, then whispered frantically, "We've already made it this far. We can't go back to your house. We'd be punished for leaving."

Neil turned a worried look back to the city behind them. "Could live...there." His voice scratched with more rasp than tone. He motioned with his head, then whispered, "No restrictions."

Katie's knees shook. She watched the gate, not him.

He wasn't wrong. Mr. Alcott may find them if they lived in the city, but he also knew where her village was and could find them there. Neil was an adult citizen with no restrictions; he could probably get a house, continue his job, or find a new one. She could still go to school. She could have exactly what she had wanted and do what Mr. Blackwell had suggested. Marry Neil, start a new life, never return.

Her eyes filled. All she wanted was her sister back. At this point she'd be thrilled to lay eyes on Jeremy. And Clark. Clark was a gap in her heart that all Neil's company couldn't fill. He was a constant draw, no matter how far away he was. No matter how incompatible their futures, how much pain their relationship brought to the table, or how severe the potential difficulties it presented might be. The gate doubled, then blurred.

"Please Neil," she whispered. "We have to try."

Neil's hand slipped back into hers, but it didn't tighten. He sighed, then tugged her toward the back of the line. Her tears dropped as she turned her face toward him, wishing he was as blurred as the gate. Surely if this went sour, only she would be taken. He could go live by himself. He'd be free. That counted for something, didn't it?

His face didn't twitch, didn't show any tinge beyond a neutral mask, but his hand began to tremble as they grew closer to the gate. But the process looked easy. Most people flashed their wrists and were waved through without question. One or two showed a box they carried or gestured toward their companion. But it looked like one person identifying themselves was enough, at least in a few cases.

Katie relaxed a little, but Neil's tremble grew into a shake as they neared the fence, and it greeted them with a buzzing hum. Now she was squeezing his hand, rethinking her own choice, but they were too close to the guards to whisper.

And then the guard was looking at her. "ID?"

Neil held out his wrist again and the voice from the box at the gate announced: "Neil Alcott. Simulator landscape programmer. Address: Number three on street B. Citizenship Class A. No restrictions."

The announcement had little effect on the man. He eyed Katie, then motioned toward her. "Is she chipped?"

"She is mine," Neil repeated.

"Is she chipped?" the man repeated, spatting each word.

"No."

The guard's eyes lit with interest. "How did you get her?"

"Gift."

"How much do you want for her?"

"She is mine."

"Come on, everybody's got a price. Will you take seventy-five UCs?"

"No."

"A hundred then?"

"She's not for sale!" Neil growled.

The guard's jaw jutted to one side. His eye scraped down her body. "Will you rent her for an hour?"

Confusion broke through Neil's face. Katie squeezed his hand harder than before.

"Give me an hour, and I'll wave your exit fee," the man said.

Panic began a steady build in Katie's chest. They'd brought no money. But Neil offered his wrist again. "She is my mate."

Katie winced at the term, but the guard only glared. The man lifted his own wrist and held it above Neil's, eliciting an even higher beep. A voice that sounded exactly like AIDA announced, "Ten universal currency coins requested from Neil Alcott. Entry transaction complete. Have a good day, Mr. Alcott. Would you like to hear your balance?"

Neil froze. The skin pulled tight against his throat, but he managed to open his lips. Confusion crossed his face again, and he cocked his head before he said, "Yes."

"Your most recent deposit was one week ago for $2,286 UCs," AIDA announced pleasantly. "Your reserve is $1,198,976 UCs."

Neil's eyes widened at the amount. He sagged, caught himself, and re-masked his face. Even the guard looked startled. His eyes sparked before he wiped the interest away with a blink. He hit a button, and the gate opened behind him. "Have a good day, Mr. Alcott. Let me know if I can find someone to assist you at any time."

Neil only offered him a stern look that mirrored the senior Mr. Alcott. He tugged Katie through. They cleared the fence, and the land opened in front of them. Rows of cars lined up, hiding tables and the merchants. Beyond that, the open fields led to the sweeping limbs of a forest of weather-beaten oak trees and scrub brush.

And past that, home.

But AIDA's speaker could be heard by anyone within twenty-five feet. Consequently, every eye lifted toward them as they walked through the gate.

"I thought you didn't get paid for your work," Katie whispered.

"Me too," Neil answered.

"You didn't know you had that money?"

He shook his head. "No, but..."

"But what..."

He blinked. "Dad is paid...each week. At $2,286, there should...be more."

"When did you start working?" Katie asked.

"Fourteen."

She frowned. There was no way of knowing for sure if he was paid every week or if he'd always earned the same amount. With the way the merchants were eyeing him, it seemed that amount was impressive, even for the city. But he kept frowning, so she asked, "Do you think...your parents?"

He shrugged, but his jaw clenched as he directed his glare toward the merchants around them. Katie lifted herself on her toes, peering for Tucker's truck. She had five seconds of a clear, but unproductive view before they were swarmed.

Neil pulled her against his chest, though she wasn't certain if he meant to protect her or shield himself. She waited for him to roar, to order them back as Mr. Alcott had, then realized...he couldn't. So she raised her own voice, yelling into the crowd. "Stand back! You will not touch us! You will not speak if you have any hope of a sale!"

It startled everyone, including Neil, but he took the chance to drag her between the men directly ahead, plowing a path through the crowd. But the merchants followed, speaking rather than shouting, still trying to list off the things they could offer.

Neil lifted his arm, knocking aside a trucker who stumbled a few steps before he recovered without so much as a complaint. But the others fell back an inch.

Katie spun, peering, but every man was taller than her and she could only see a sea of chests, shoulders, and dingy clothes; some covered in holes, others only dust.

"Go!" Neil called, then coughed. His breathing grew trapped and increasingly ragged, but he croaked again. "Leave us...alone!"

And then above the clammer a familiar voice called, "Katie?"

Her head jerked around, seeing only a sea of stubbled faces and nostrils, but she gathered the biggest breath she could and screamed, "Tucker!"

From the edge of the circle, men stumbled aside as Tucker roared, "Leave 'em alone, you scumbags! Back to your booths and let them breathe!"

She wasn't sure if the group listened to his shout or the speaker that boomed from the fence. "Every merchant to his booth!"

The crowd broke up, leaving her gasping for fresh air. Neil clung to her, his entire body so ridged even his shaking was restricted to a tight tremble.

Tucker strode up with a grin, sweeping his eyes from her to the man standing behind her. "Well, it's about time, girl!"

"Back to your booth," the guard behind them yelled.

Tucker threw an irritated look but waved at the pair to follow him. "I've been looking for you every market day. I didn't know if my poor heart could handle going back to your sister again with no letter."

Katie jogged to catch up with him. "How long has it been?"

"Four months." Tucker peeked toward her. "Who you got with you?"

"This is Neil."

"Well, I heard that from the speaker. Neil, you a college boy too?"

"No," Katie answered. She glanced at the other merchants. A few were engaging customers, but most stood at desolate booths eyeing Neil with hungry eyes. She dropped her voice to an urgent whisper. "Tucker, we need you to get us out of here. I'll explain everything on the road, but we need to leave right now."

The man frowned. "How come? You guys in some kind of trouble?"

"There is no college," Katie said. "I don't think there ever was a scholarship."

Tucker turned his head to stare at her. "What?"

"My sponsors locked me inside their house the day I got there."

"That couple I gave you to?" Tucker sputtered.

"Yeah."

"Oh, no, I ain't that kind of man! They didn't pay me nothing for you!"

"I know it wasn't you. They're just evil people, and they tricked us. Neil helped me escape, but they're going to be looking for us." Her voice cracked as she begged, "Mr. Alcott can't find us, Tucker. We have to get out of here."

"Oh, he'd better not show up here." Tucker shook his head. "I'll put a fist right though his face!"

"Then you'll get arrested, and we'll still be stuck," Katie said, because Neil's breath was beginning to pick up. "Can't you just take us to the village?"

"I will, but I gotta pack up my stuff," Tucker grimaced as he spoke. "Half of it I'm selling for other people. I don't even own it."

Katie nodded. "Okay. You load up. Neil and I will pretend to look at the booths, so we don't attract too much attention."

"Good plan," Tucker said.

Katie took Neil's hand, frowning to feel it still trembling. Tucker picked up one of the unopened crates and casually carried it to the bed of the truck while they hovered in front of his booth.

She swallowed, suddenly realizing it was almost a museum of her little village. She touched the stack of cloth. "See this? This is made from cotton me and my sister grew."

Neil cocked his head, touching first it, then touched the jars of canned corn.

"That's corn. My friend, Allison? Her family grows it."

Tucker eyed them as he made trips to the truck.

She glanced back but said nothing until Neil wandered on his own to the next booth. Katie grabbed two jars of corn to walk beside Tucker, nesting it back into the crate.

"Who is this Neil person?" Tucker asked.

Katie swallowed, hating to lie. "He was locked in the house when I got there. He's been a slave there most of his life."

"Was he bought or stolen?"

"Does it matter?"

"It matters for me," Tucker said. "If they legally own him, I'm looking at being caught with stolen goods."

"They don't legally own him," Katie said. "No more than me."

"Where's his family?"

"Neil's been alone since he was a child," Katie replied carefully. "He doesn't have anybody but me."

He sucked in a breath like he was contemplating the repercussions of taking a city person away from the inborder. But he nodded. "A friend of yours is a friend of mine."

"Thank you," Katie whispered.

He gave her a sideways glance. "I'm supposing you've moved on from Clark then?"

Katie froze.

Swallowed, then evaded with a question, "How is Clark?"

"Dutiful son by day. Black market water-deliverer by night." Tucker set down another crate and lifted his hands. "But you didn't hear that from me."

Katie stared. "He's stealing water? How long has he done that?"

"He's done it for years." Tucker raised his eyebrows toward her as they returned to the table to box up the jars. "I thought you knew."

She shook her head.

"Well, most people don't. They just know the water shows up in their bucket like it was left by fairies. I only know because I caught him."

Katie took a breath. "Please don't...I'll figure out what to tell him about Neil."

Tucker's mouth pulled farther down. "Have you told Neil about Clark?"

"I told Neil what he needed to know so we could escape."

"Don't you think you should, before you haul him to the outborder?"

"I told Neil if he helped me get away, he could live in the village, and nobody would hurt him anymore. All he wants is a place to belong." She moved away before Tucker had a chance to respond, sucking in a breath as she walked to the booth where the merchant was talking so much Neil couldn't get a word in edgewise if he'd wanted to.

He was calmer now and sent her a soft smile. The merchant was smiling too. Neil must have bought something. It was weird to see him outside. Weird to see him normal. But something in her relaxed, something she hadn't even realized was wound tight.

Neil would be fine. He would adapt to village life. He would be accepted. He would, eventually, forgive her. But she couldn't tell him, not now, not yet. He wouldn't come if she did. Figuring out how to buy something at a market didn't constitute knowing how to live on his own. If she went without him, his parents would find him. They'd lock him back up.

Clark would understand.

Neil took her hand, held it in place and piled in a delicate golden necklace. "For me?" she asked.

He nodded.

She willed her face not to flush. Offered him a smile. "Thank you."

The pendent was two garnets set in gold rings that interlocked. Neil took it back, draped it around her neck, and she stood while he fumbled with the clasp. It was the sort of thing she'd once dreamed of wearing back to the village. The sort of thing even Clark's family would struggle to afford.

She felt Tucker's curious glance, along with the smile of the merchant who looked as though he liked young love as well as money.

What was she going to do? She couldn't have both Clark and Neil. She pulled the worry from her face, and wrapped her fingers around the gift, now the owner of two red gems held together by chains.

The Reunion

THE CLOSER SHE GOT to home, the more she worried about the entire village coming out and overwhelming Neil. She also hadn't figured out what to tell Mr. Blackwell about her decision to return—with or without his approval.

"Tucker, can you take us to Jeremy's farm the back way?" she asked. "I don't want the entire village coming at once."

"Neither do I," Tucker fretted. "They're going to wonder why I still have all their things."

Neil nudged her leg, whispering, "I'll buy."

"Can you do that?" Katie asked.

Neil nodded.

"Do what?" Tucker asked.

"He wants to buy the whole load, but I don't know how much that would cost."

Tucker threw her a glance. "Sweetheart, Neil's got enough money to buy the entire market. But we're going to keep that between the three of us. Nobody in town needs to know that, least of all Mr. Blackwell."

Neil's eyebrows pinched but he said, "Give to family."

"Mallory and Jeremy?" Katie asked.

Neil nodded, then turned his face toward the window, watching the trees rush by. It was winter now, and the grass was dead. The mesquite trees maintained their tiny leaves, but the thorns offered a sinister look. Katie swallowed. December was dreary, but January and February could be brutal, and she wasn't sure how Neil would handle three months of cold and hunger. She'd have to tell him all about spring.

But Jeremy would have meat at least, though she was sure he'd planned for two people, not four. Of course, Neil could purchase food, but it didn't seem fair to take advantage, not unless they were truly together.

She felt helpless and tears pricked.

She refused to look down the road that led to her old house as they passed it, afraid to witness its fate.

Jeremy's house was close now, and her heart sped.

Neil tore his eyes from the window to glance at her, sensing her squirm.

She sent him what she hoped was a convincing smile. "Almost there."

And then they were there. Jeremy and Mallory were strolling from the barn, both carrying feed buckets. Mallory cocked her head toward the truck, said something to Jeremy. Then spied Katie and dropped both of her buckets, spilling corn over the ground.

Katie climbed over Neil, and Tucker barely got the truck stopped before she jumped out, bracing herself as Mallory barreled toward her.

"Katie!" Mallory's arms wrapped around her, and her sister squeezed so tight Katie couldn't move. "We were beginning to think we'd never see you again! Are you on school break?"

Katie had planned on explaining things calmly, but now that it came to the moment, all she could do was cry.

"Katie..." Mallory's voice changed.

She didn't see their stares, but she heard Jeremy setting down his buckets, Neil's breathing strained and slow behind her, and Tucker shifting in the creaking seat.

"Katie's been all locked up this whole time," Tucker said.

"What?" Mallory sputtered.

Katie felt her sister's chin lift to stare at the man, but she only tightened her grip on her sister.

"Where?" Jeremy asked. "At the school?"

And Neil's voice, low and somber, finally confirming what she'd feared. "There's...no school. It's a lie."

"A lie?" Mallory sputtered. "Katie got a scholarship."

"Not true." Neil said. "Trick. To find...someone with...no family."

"She has a family!" Mallory snapped. She pulled back from Katie, but only to stroke her hair back behind her ears.

"Wait," Jeremy asked. "Who are you?"

Katie pulled back quickly, opening her mouth as she glanced back to Neil.

"Neil helped me get away," Katie said and found his eyes as she spoke. "He's the *only* reason I got away. Mallory, they can't find us."

"Do they know you're here?" Mallory asked.

"No. Maybe they'll guess, but they won't show up after kidnapping me, will they? It's illegal here, even if it's not in the city."

Mallory cast a worried glanced toward her husband. Katie's heart seized with a sudden fear.

But the man's eyebrows only drew in concern before he said, "Why don't you all come inside, and we'll talk over lunch? I'll finish the feeding, and then you can tell the whole story."

"I've got to get this all unloaded," Tucker said, thumbing toward the bed of his truck where crates peeked haphazardly over the edge.

"Oh, um." Katie swallowed. "Neil bought all of Tucker's stuff so we could get out quickly, so it's all going inside."

"What?" Jeremy asked. "We don't need all this."

"Well, it's paid for," Tucker said. "So I can leave it in your yard, or I can unload it in your house, but I ain't bringing people their money with the things still in my truck. I don't need that kind of talk."

Jeremy frowned but offered a nod. "Well...okay."

Neil glanced between the men and Katie but climbed out and began to unload the crates. Katie tried to catch his eye, but his face had become closed and clouded again. Mallory took her hand and towed her to the house. "We'll pull some lunch together."

By the speed and force of the journey, lunch wasn't the only thing she wanted to pull together. She opened the door, and they stepped directly into the kitchen where the smell of bread made Katie instantly weak.

Mallory dropped her hand but only to hold her face in something between a caress and a clamp, like she was afraid Katie was going to lie. "Did they hurt you?"

"No," Katie answered. "I mean...not really."

"Who is that man?"

"He's..." Katie stalled. "His name is Neil. He was there when I got there. They made him do a certain amount of work every day, and they punished him if he didn't get it done."

"So he's a slave, too?"

"Yeah," Katie's answer wavered.

Her sister eyed her. "Are you...together?"

Katie's answer twisted in her head, suddenly afraid if she said no, the couple wasn't going to extend their protection to Neil. Certainly, Mallory wasn't going to put up with any sort of facade about liking one man while appearing to date another. "No," she said. "They wanted us to be. They brought me to be his companion, but we're not together."

Her eyes filled, and Mallory's gaze softened. "Did he...take advantage of you?"

Katie shook her head. "No. He could have. But he didn't. Neil has..."

But there wasn't time to make a case for Neil's character because the door opened again.

Tucker crossed the threshold with a crate full of jars of corn. Neil followed with the box of material but hesitated at the door. He swallowed and stepped through, kneeling to set down the crate. Katie began to talk to him, but he hurried out before one word was said.

Mallory frowned. "He bought all of this?"

"He wanted to make sure everyone got paid."

"Katie, we can't afford to pay him back."

"It's a gift," Katie said. "He came up with the idea. Please just take it. He won't miss the money, but he's scared. He's not used to kind people."

"How does he have money? I thought he was locked up."

"He was, but he wasn't supposed to be."

"Katie, that doesn't make sense."

"I can't tell you everything about Neil. He doesn't talk well, so I don't even know everything about Neil. All I can tell you is that there's no way I would be here if it wasn't for him. He saved my life, four different times."

"He saved your life?" Mallory echoed.

Katie covered her face as a fresh bout of tears came, because now she'd said too much. Now her sister was going to have to know the whole truth about the shocks and the lies and the coaxing it had taken to convince Neil to leave his home. "They're going to do horrible things to Neil if they find him. I told him if he could help me get here, nobody would hurt him anymore. Every time I tried to escape, they punished him."

Mallory crushed her in a hug again and whispered, "Gracious, Katie."

"You can't send him away, Mallory. You can't."

"Nobody said anything about sending him away," Mallory answered. She pulled in a deep breath, whispering more to herself than Katie. "Okay." She pulled back. "We're going to help the guys put all this stuff in the pantry. And then we're going to sit down and talk things out."

Katie nodded, only slightly more reassured. She forced the tears back and grabbed the first crate that came inside, taking it from Jeremy without looking at his face.

Even with Mallory's scrupulous housekeeping, the kitchen walls were covered with faded paint with bits peeled off and smoothed away. An entire wall was dedicated to hanging herbs, and a loaf of bread peeked from a glass covering on the table. The fire flickered behind the screen where an aluminum kettle steamed.

She wondered what Neil would make of it, but his eyes only gave a quick rove as he set down another crate and rushed back to the doorway, looking paler with each trip. When the truck was emptied, he offered his wrist again to the machine plugged into Tucker's truck, completing the transaction.

Tucker declined lunch, opting to go to the bank to exchange the UCs into the town currency.

Katie stepped closer to Neil as the truck rolled away. "Come inside and eat."

Neil shook his head. "No doors."

Katie paused. "Neil, they're not going to lock us inside."

Neil's eyes glinted again, and he choked, "No doors."

Katie sighed but turned to shout, "Mallory, can we eat outside for lunch?"

"Outside?" Mallory called back.

"It's not very cold. I've been locked in a house for four months."

Neil threw her a grateful look, but he still squirmed.

Mallory appeared with a plate of sandwiches. "Well, I suppose we can. Since you put it that way."

By the time Jeremy came in from the pigs, the girls had a blanket on the ground and plates of food set around like it was a spring picnic. A curious smile pulled at the man's mouth, but he asked no questions as he sat next to his wife.

Katie told the story as simply as she could: Neil was kept inside and required to do a certain amount of work each day. She was brought to keep him company. They had been left alone, planned an escape, and he'd broken down the door and helped her navigate the city. Guilt pricked at the omissions, but she'd satisfied Mallory's curiosity for how Neil had saved her life, and he'd squirmed so much at the tale of the first escape that she'd kept the details to the scolding and starvation because neither of them wanted to relive the truth.

She made no mention of AIDA, nor Neil's last name, or the detail that he hadn't exactly planned any escape. Neil stayed quiet, offering no protest to the story, but his head swiveled toward the rustling trees, the squeal of the pigs, the distant barking of a dog. There was no pretending in the building nerves of the man who'd never seen anything beyond four walls.

Mallory grew pale but attempted to pick up the conversation, pulling the boy back in. "What kind of work did you do, Neil?"

Neil's head snapped back. He blinked. "I...build worlds."

"Build worlds?"

"On the screen."

"He's kind of an artist," Katie said. "He makes pictures that move. It's something they do in the city."

"What are they for?" Jeremy asked.

"I don't know." Katie turned to Neil. "Do you even know?"

Neil shook his head and shrugged.

"Well, what else can you do?" Jeremy asked.

Neil blinked. "...build little worlds...on the table."

"I imagine he could do just about anything if it doesn't require a lot of talking," Katie said. "He's a quick learner."

Jeremy nodded once. "Well, I guess he can always help me with the pigs until he finds somewhere to work."

"Pigs?" Neil asked.

"It's a kind of animal," Mallory explained.

"It's bacon," Katie said, and Neil stared.

"We'll have to find work for you too, Katie, now that you are both staying," Mallory said. She gathered the empty plates as she spoke, pretending not to notice that even Neil sagged a bit in relief at the implications. "Maybe you could help Kathrine at the dress shop. She's been struggling to keep up with the orders for winter clothes."

Katie nodded slowly. She'd been so set on getting home, she hadn't thought about what she'd do when she got here. "I'll ask her," she said. "We'll need to get some clothes anyway. They took mine, and we didn't bring any."

Mallory nodded. "We'll go tomorrow. Everyone will want to see you anyway."

The story had worked. Mallory was going to let them stay. Katie sneaked a glance at Jeremy, but his face showed more sadness than fear. She swallowed, vowing that she would tell the whole truth later.

But did it matter, really? She was home. The Alcott's had broken the law, at least the local ones by trying to steal her. Surely, they wouldn't risk charges by coming.

AIDA was broken and there was no electricity here to control Neil. And she was pretty sure, even in the inborder where people got away with importing slaves, that they weren't allowed to lock grown children inside and torture work out of them. Neil didn't even know he was making income, and he thought there should be more, which meant they were possibly spending his without telling him.

At this point, they should say nothing and hope Neil and Katie never pressed charges. So she had nothing to worry about, right?

Her sister turned back to drink the last of her water glass. Katie swallowed, remembering Mr. Blackwell's reminder that he owned the well her sister drank from.

Well, maybe she had one thing to worry about.

Surely, Mr. Blackwell was bluffing. Jeremy may be a pig farmer, but he was well-liked in town. And Mr. Blackwell wasn't going to risk offending Neil if he got wind of how much the boy was able to pay for Tucker's load.

She glanced at Neil, embarrassed that she once again felt shielded by him. Resolving that, as far as she could help it, Mr. Blackwell would never know. But if he didn't, would he come after Jeremy?

She swallowed the worry. She'd find a solution. Jeremy couldn't be the second man to suffer for her choices.

Hope Rises

"ARE YOU SURE YOU WANT to sleep here?" Katie asked as she tucked the blanket's edge beneath the hay. "It's going to get colder."

Neil motioned toward the quilt that sat folded near the ladder to the loft.

"It may not be enough," Katie warned. "We'll leave the house door unlocked, so you can come sleep by the fire if you change your mind."

Who knew? Neil would probably tolerate winter better than summer and the barn did look cozy, even with the open loft door. That, she suspected, was what Neil was after: the big square of open air between him and the stars that, apparently, he no longer felt were watching.

"Stay?" Neil asked.

Katie shook her head. "No, I can't. Mallory wouldn't allow it."

It was true. But it wasn't the real reason, and she winced as Neil's eyebrows drew. She'd spent almost all day trying to convince Neil that Mallory and Jeremy weren't threats, and now she was throwing rules at him like they were in charge.

But it was their house. And Mallory had grown up as the scandalous child who'd settled a romantic feud. She wasn't going to be keen on Katie sleeping next to any guy, boyfriend or not. Clark wouldn't be thrilled about it either.

Katie resisted a sigh and sent him a smile. "I'll see you in the morning."

By the time she'd reached the ladder, Neil's eyes had already returned to the moonlit yard. He should be fine. He couldn't wander off too far without proper light, and she doubted he would try. The door would be locked, so wild animals couldn't get into the barn.

She couldn't stay with him. That would be sending mixed signals. Now that she was home, she didn't have to pretend anymore. Her job wasn't keeping Neil happy. She didn't have a job at all. She walked through the yard, hugging herself. She'd thought when she'd gotten home, life would resolve, but it seemed she'd only traded one set of problems for another.

And then a whisper came out of the dark. "Katie?"

She gasped but used the same breath to squeal, "Clark!"

She saw his outline, felt his arms wrap around her. He felt short now, when he never had before, but it was a good size, a few inches taller than herself and comfortable, not looming. He smelled like the rest of her villagers, like sun and rain and the faintest floral hint of the inside of his home. He squeezed her, and he felt like her father had, a taut layer of muscles smoothing the ridges of his ribs. He was thinner than she remembered.

"Katie, I'm so sorry!" he whispered. "I should have known something was wrong! I should have come look for you."

"You wouldn't have found me," Katie said. She frowned. "Tucker told you?"

"Tucker? No," he said. "Tucker didn't breathe a word, even when I begged him to tell. All that I got out of him was that they lied about the scholarship. Aunt Bonnie thought she saw you ride past in his truck. She told Dad you were probably just on a break, but he's furious. That's why I couldn't come until now." His teeth clenched slightly. "I couldn't even go to the porch without someone asking where I was going."

"What is wrong with them?" Katie hissed. "They have no right to say whether or not I can live in the village!"

"It's us, Katie," Clark said. "Dad doesn't want you with me. But he'll calm down, and I think I figured out a way without waiting for him to die."

Katie closed her eyes, almost afraid to hear. "How?"

"You can't tell anyone yet, not even Mallory."

"Okay."

"Remember that hermit that lives on the edge of the creek who used to yell at us to quit eating his pears?"

"Yes."

"His name is Mr. Maton. He had a stroke out in his orchard, and I've been going out to check on him. We've become friends. He told me when he was little and the Blackout first started, most of the families drank from the river. You could, back then. But his grandfather drilled and found an artesian well on their land. They kept it a secret for almost forty years until it collapsed in on itself."

"So there's another well in town?" Katie asked.

"Not yet, but there could be," Clark said. "He doesn't have any children, or any family left at all. I told him I'd buy the land from him, if he'd let me pay in installments. I've been paying him in supplies to make him as comfortable as he likes. I was worried still, that I couldn't pay enough before he dies. I think it's only a year or maybe less with his health going down. But he said last week that he put in his will that the land was to go to me because he's got no use for it after he's gone. And once we get a well, Father can't control everyone anymore. At least, not with threats about water."

"What about Jeremy and Mallory?" Katie asked. She swallowed and admitted, "Your father told me when I left that he didn't want me to come back and, if I did, he'd stop selling Jeremy water."

"He ranted about that today too, but I'm not sure he actually will," Clark said. "He's got the water, but Jeremy has the pigs. Even if he does, I'll get water to you. I'm not going to let anything bad happen to you again, not if I can help it."

Her older, wiser self knew better: there was no way he could make such a promise, not in a world where even the police tried to buy her. But she wanted to believe it, because he was Clark, because they'd finally ended this dance of denial, because somehow Clark always found a way.

She lifted her face; her lips went straight to his. He jolted in surprise, but he wrapped his arms around her to pull her closer. It was nothing like she'd imagined her first kiss being, but a thrill went through her. She'd gotten it all wrong, but it still felt right.

And then Mallory ruined it, calling from the doorway. "Katie!"

Katie and Clark both huffed a laugh.

She pushed him away, slowly. "Go for now. No one knows we're together."

"But we are together?" Clark whispered.

"Yes."

He kissed her again, impulsively, and then disappeared into the shadows of the trees.

Katie's smile grew in the dark, even after he left. Her city shoes crunched against the crushed leaves and dry grass, but it was a comforting sound. She wasn't sure how things would work out, but they would. Somehow, she and Clark would make sure that they would. She bit her lip against a grin and returned to her sister's house.

The Betrayal

KATIE WOKE AND STARED at the rafters as reality replaced her nightmares. She was at Jeremy's home. Neil was sleeping in the barn. And Clark had promised her a future together. She wondered if life would have had the same outcome if she had never gone to the city or if her absence had helped both of them realize what they truly wanted. Maybe something good would come out of her captivity. And at least Neil was free. His parents would have gone on tricking him for the rest of his life if they hadn't decided to trick her.

She smelled bacon and grinned to herself. How much had changed. Maybe the promise of familiar food would lure Neil into the house, at least for an hour. Katie shoved back the blankets, dressed in her blue city dress, and padded through the kitchen and down the porch steps barefooted.

The sun was up, but the sky was still turning from pink to blue. She glanced over the yard, spying Jeremy in the far pasture surrounded by pigs.

Clark was right. Jeremy's farm was nothing fancy, but he ran it well. She could see the layers of replaced boards overlapping the peeling original paint. But Jeremy *had* replaced them, keeping his home as tidy as the limited supplies in the town allowed.

She wondered what state the old hermit's cabin was in. It didn't matter. She and Clark would fix it up and live there, hopefully with water bubbling up nearby.

"Neil!" she called, stepping into the doorway.

There was no reply, but Neil was a hard sleeper, so she didn't panic until she reached the top of the ladder and found only an empty indent in the blanket. She stepped down the rungs and circled the barn to the pig pens where Jeremy was mixing rainwater into buckets of corn.

"Jeremy, have you seen Neil?"

Jeremy straightened, then thumbed toward the woods. "He left at sunup, headed toward the river."

"What? Why didn't you stop him?"

"He's a grown man," Jeremy said. "He's just exploring."

"He's never been out of the house!" Katie cried.

"And he thinks I'm going to lock him inside of mine," Jeremy said. "If he wants to leave my yard, and I try to stop him, what do you think is going to happen?"

"He doesn't know anything about the woods! He's going to step in a trap!"

Jeremy shook his head. "No, I showed him where the trail was and told him to be sure and stay on it so he could find his way back. He'll be all right."

"I'm gonna find him," Katie said. "Breakfast is ready anyway."

"Better put on some shoes."

"Trust me. Bare feet are better than the shoes I have."

"Better get some good ones from town."

"I will after I find Neil."

And a job so she could pay her brother-in-law back for the new sets of clothes. She stepped carefully, but the path was well-worn, and she made good time following it to the river. She'd envisioned every scenario that could have gone wrong: days with search parties trying to rescue Neil if he'd wandered off or finding him with a foot caught up in a trap. Surely, he wouldn't try to eat anything, right?

But, at the end of the path, there he was, relaxing beside the river, and he'd even had the good sense to sit on a log instead of the red clay at the base of the cliffs. He stood as she stepped onto the path.

Terror brushed his face, before he grinned and motioned her toward him.

"Neil, you sca—"

"Shh!" Neil held his finger to his lip. Half his mouth lifted in the sudden smile that one wears when they stumble on a fellow countryman in a foreign country. He lifted his hand, pointing upward behind her.

She swiveled, scanning the cliff until red clay met blue sky. Then on a lower ledge, not twenty feet away, she glimpsed a flash of movement. Tawny fur outlined a feline shape against the rocks, smooth flesh blocking out the rough crevices.

The golden eyes of a young mountain lion locked onto hers. The animal pulled its ears against his head, carefully placing each paw in front of the other, taking slow, measured steps toward them. Katie opened her mouth to shout. Her dehydrated vocal cords clashed, squeaked, choked.

The creature locked its eyes onto her. Stepped into the dried clay.

Katie stumbled backward, then crashed into Neil's chest. She felt his arms catch her. He stepped, dragging her, back, back, back. His shoe hit her heel. She felt him tilt. She landed on his chest, feeling his breath slam against the back of her neck.

She rolled off his chest onto her stomach and pushed herself halfway up. Paws hit her shoulders. Her arms collapsed. Her face slammed into the ground. A rock pressed into her cheek, drawing blood as a heavier weight landed on her back, crushing out her breath. She thought at first it was Neil, until the teeth grazed her neck.

Just as suddenly, the weight lifted. She crawled out from beneath the mountain lion and stumbled to her feet. Her hand went to her neck, squishing warm blood against her skin. She spun.

Neil was on his side, squeezing the creature's neck. He straddled its back, his top leg gripping the creature's ribs, his bottom trapped beneath its weight. The mountain lion turned its head toward Neil, snapping his teeth near his face.

A scream found its way past Katie's dry cords, ripping into the air. She grabbed a branch and slammed it across the creature's snout. The branch busted, sending a shower of bark into Neil's face. She danced out of the way as the claws flailed, the mountain lion swiping the air. Neil clung on, grunting between growls.

"Hey!" A yell rang from the trees. It sounded like Clark, only louder and rougher than she'd ever heard. A gun exploded from the trees at the top of the cliff.

Neil jumped and the cat bucked, pulling free from Neil's legs. Their bodies broke apart, creating a V as the creature tried to back out of his choke hold.

Clark slid down the slope of the cliff, landing next to Katie, leveling his pistol at the pair on the ground. His finger tightened on the trigger, but he hesitated, his eyebrows twisted in concentration as he aimed his barrel toward the two heads. He swung the barrel high, fired again into the air.

The animal twisted above Neil, sliding free of his grasp. It ran toward the cliffs leaving Neil pawing the air, then shielding his face.

Clark swung the pistol, following the animal's flight, waiting until the mountain lion was farther away from Neil.

The explosion jerked the animal's head to one side. His face went down first, hitting the dirt, dragging the nose beneath his chest, then falling into a heap.

Clark sent a second bullet into the creature, gaining no reaction from the animal. Then he lowered the gun, swinging toward her. "Katie? Are you okay?"

She clung to him, shaking, now that the animal was dead. Her back hurt from the claws, her ribs aching from the crushing fall. But she took two breaths, finding that everything still worked as it should.

Clark lowered his head, and his chin was rough with stubble now. She didn't want to leave his arms, but she nodded and stepped away from him to check Neil.

Neil pushed himself up, resting on one leg, then twisted away from them to peer at the tufts of fur that rustled in the wind. Then slowly turned back, blinking toward Clark and his gun. His face slacked, realization quickly being replaced by terror. He surged to his feet, his eyes trained on the weapon like it was the same device that controlled AIDA.

Clark leveled his barrel at Neil, barking, "Who are you?"

"Stop!" Katie sputtered. "Stop, Clark, he's a friend."

But Neil stood with both fists clenched, heaving deep breaths, moving a glare from Clark to the dead animal nearby. His clothes were stained with the dust from the red clay. Blood trickle from a slash in his left arm. His eyes held a primitive glint.

"Neil?" Katie asked. She took a sidestep away from Clark, talking like she would to a spooked horse. "It's okay, Neil. That lion was going to eat you. He only shot it because he had to. He's not going to shoot us." Katie took three steps forward toward Neil, putting herself between them, speaking as evenly as she could manage. "Clark, this is Neil. He's never seen a gun."

"What?" Clark sputtered.

Katie's voice began to shake. "Clark, put down the gun. Please."

Neil's chest heaved harder with each breath. He held his hand toward Katie. She took another step to appease him.

"Neil, this is my friend, Clark Blackwell. You remember. I told you about him."

Neil's eyebrow twitched once, but hers tucked as she tried to remember exactly what she'd told him. Most of the time, she'd omitted Clark from the picture she'd painted of home.

She listened for the shifting of metal behind, but all she heard was Clark's voice. "Katie, come back."

"Clark, please put the gun down. He's just scared."

Neil stood with his fists clenched and chest heaving. His eyes slit, his face contorted with pain, fear, and full-on hatred.

"Scared? He's acting like an animal, Katie," Clark said.

"He's not an animal!" Katie snapped. "He doesn't understand our world!"

Neil winced, turning a surprised look toward her.

She heard the click of Clark's hammer being slowly maneuvered into a neutral position. "Can he understand us?"

"Yes. But they hurt his throat, so it's hard for him to talk."

Clark sucked in a slow breath, but he lowered the rifle to rest the butt on the ground.

Neil turned his full attention to Katie's face. He held out his hand again, but she hesitated, regretting the action when his stare turned into a series of blinks.

If Clark was looking for signs of humanity, the next five seconds showed them all: the glaze of confusion, slump of betrayal, and lines of pain finally etching into to every crevice of his face.

The Apprentice

KATIE'S HEELS WOBBLED over the loose debris in the road. She comforted herself that the trip back from town would be easier in the new boots. But she was glad for the chance to walk because the adrenaline was still coursing through her body.

Clark had managed to calm himself down, even risking leaving his rifle hidden near the river while he helped Katie coax Neil back to the house. Neil had calmed too, though she suspected that it had more to do with the blood seeping from between his fingers, because he wouldn't let either of them come within three feet.

Not even her, and though she had picked Clark to share her future, the rejection stung. But they still needed clothes, even more now that their outfits were stained with red clay and blood.

"Katie, he'll be all right," Jeremy said. "It's not a deep wound. Mallory can stitch it up, probably, now that we're not there."

Katie continued her brisk pace, but it only required her brother-in-law to slightly lengthen his gait. Her back was sore.

Katie rubbed a tear away. "I know. I just wish he would have let Clark help him."

"Well, he's only been here two days. You can't expect him to trust everyone. Give him some time." Jeremy stuck his hands into his pockets and sent her a sidelong glance. "It's going to take a bit to adapt. Even you are coming back to a different life."

"I *feel* different, but not in a good way." Her eyes filled. "And now he's seen Clark, and I don't know what to do."

"What do you want to do?"

Katie sucked in a breath, looking past her brother-in-law to the barn of one of the Blackwell farms. "I want to be with Clark."

"Is Clark really an option though?"

"Clark proposed to me," Katie said. "Before I left and again last night. And I told him yes."

Jeremy's eyebrows climbed, but he kept his easy gait. "Well, a yes for Clark is a no for Neil."

"But Neil gave up everything for me," Katie said. "They brought me for him, but when I tried to escape, they were going to sell me again or kill me. Neil wouldn't let them, and they punished him because of me. And he just..." Her voice changed to a whisper like her mind was resisting telling the secret. "He just let them. He broke down the door, he got me through the gate, he kept the men from buying me. And I promised that if he didn't like it here, I'd go back with him. I didn't want to lie but I..." She trailed off, too choked to continue.

Jeremy pushed his hands into his pockets, studying the ground as they walked. "But you needed him to get away."

"Yeah." Katie pressed the heel of her hand against her eye. "I have made terrible things happen to Neil. When I tried to leave that house, Neil said I hated him because I tried to go alone. And he was right—about the leaving—but not the hating. I didn't want him to be hurt, I just didn't know if he would go. And then I promised him all these things he'd get here if he came, so he'd break down the door."

"Did you promise to marry him?" Jeremy asked.

"No. I said he could live here, and he wouldn't be alone because he could be part of our village. But I didn't...I didn't really say I wouldn't marry him. And I kind of let him assume we were together. But I don't hate him. I just...don't love him. But I owe him."

Jeremy's eyes were shaded beneath the brim of his hat, but he shook his head. "You were being held against your will. You were doing what you thought you had to survive. I think maybe the only thing you owe Neil is the truth."

"But I don't know what the truth is going to do to him."

"It takes two people to love, Katie. And it's not love if it's based on a lie."

"But I don't know what he'll do if I tell the truth."

"Every lie has consequences. Even those we don't want to tell. But the consequences of telling the truth are never as bad as those of covering your lie with more lies."

"And then what?"

"Then you focus on Katie and becoming who Katie needs to be. And you let Neil and Clark decide who they're going to be. The only choices you can control are yours. You can't guilt someone into loving you. And you can't force them to stay."

He was right, but she wasn't ready to think about it yet. They had reached the edge of the town, and she didn't want anyone to spy her with eyes full of tears.

So she sucked in a breath, then weakly teased, "Sage advice from four months of marriage."

"I got it from my father." Jeremy's smile crept a little higher. "On the day Mallory came to school holding Gordon's hand and broke my sixteen-year-old heart."

Katie threw back her head, laughing and moaning at the same time. "Her Gordon phase! I remember that! Oh, I hated him. He was such a jerk."

"But a very handsome jerk," Jeremy countered.

Katie groaned, then shook her head as she laughed. "I am so glad she married you."

The man chuckled and stepped onto the porch of the seamstress shop. "Me too. You want me to stay with you at Katherine's?"

"No, run your errands. I'll be fine," Katie said. "Thanks."

Jeremy nodded. "Wait here when you're done. I'll swing back by."

Katie nodded and watched Jeremy walk away, worrying his steps wouldn't be so relaxed once Mr. Blackwell realized she wasn't just visiting. She blew out a breath. One truth at a time.

She pushed open the door and crept into the shop. No one browsed the shelves, and she followed the clack of the ancient sewing machine to the room in the back. She watched Katherine hum as she worked, waiting for her to finish sewing the seam before she said, "Good morning."

Katherine gasped, then grinned and shoved her chair back. "Katie! I heard a rumor you were back! It's so good to see you! I've been wondering about you!"

"I'm back." Katie forced a smile. "For good. School didn't work out so well."

"Well, I'm sorry to hear that," Katherine said. "I'm awfully glad to see you though! We worried when we didn't hear anything. Does Clark know you're back?"

"Yeah, he does."

"Good," Katherine said. "I was almost as worried about him. He never complained about it, but you could see his heart breaking into pieces everywhere he went. It's been terrible to watch."

Katie grimaced. "Yeah, I seem to have a gift for breaking hearts." She huffed a breath and then stepped back. "I had a bit of a mishap this morning and the dress is stained now, but I was hoping...maybe I could still trade it?"

"What, this dress?" Katherine blinked, gesturing toward the blue.

"It's the only one I have," Katie said. "They took my other clothes. And I need something more practical. Something for a pig farm. I don't want to spend any more of Jeremy's money than I have to."

Katherine stared at the blue dress. "That is gorgeous. What material is it?"

"I don't even know," Katie said.

Katherine cupped the side of her face with one hand and rested her elbow in the other palm in the pose she always took when working out a calculation. "I don't mind trading it, not at all. But the only dress I have that would fit you is for fall. It's a cotton, quarter-length sleeve. I do have an extra cloak you can borrow, and you'd be warm enough in that, I think, until we could get you a winter dress."

"Anything is better than this," Katie said. "But I don't want to take your cloak."

"Too bad." Katherine grinned at her. "I have two, and you have none. And a person can only wear one cloak at a time. Besides, I already feel like I'm cheating you. I can sell a city dress to a Blackwell woman for quite a lot, especially if it's made from something unusual."

"Just don't tell them it was mine," Katie said. "Or they won't be caught dead in it."

"Makes it all the more fun, doesn't it?" Katherine chuckled, walking into the main room to a rack where she went through a small assortment of garments. "It's not really your coloring, but I can pick something better for the winter dress. Two dresses for the one, would be a fair trade, I think."

"I was actually wondering if I could trade it for one dress and a man's outfit?" Katie asked.

Katherine pulled a dark green dress from the rack and tipped her head toward Katie. "Intriguing."

"And I need you to keep that a secret."

"Only if you explain what secret I'm keeping."

"We have a man from the city staying with us," Katie said.

"Why must it be a secret?"

"He's...sort of a runaway slave."

Katherine's eyebrows climbed. "Is slavery legal in the city?"

"I don't know," Katie said. "But I don't think it matters. A police officer offered to buy me. And if they're buying slaves, they're not going to be protecting any. That's why you can't tell anyone."

"I won't." Katherine's eyes took a determined glint. She strode toward Katie, giving her the dress. "Here. Try this on, just in case we need to alter it. I'll find something for him. Does he have a name?"

"Neil," Katie said. "He's big."

"How big?"

"Like, find the tallest thing you possibly have, and we'll see?"

"Is he as tall as David Blackwell?"

"Taller."

"Taller?"

"He's at least six feet. Maybe a little more. But he doesn't look tall because he's wider too. He dwarfs Jeremy. And probably every other man in town."

"Good night!" Katherine exclaimed. "Are all the city men like that?"

"I don't really know," Katie said. "But Neil's father is about two inches taller than he is. I think it's because they never run out of food there."

"I'll stop by today and take his measurements," Katherine said. "If he's that big, nothing here will fit. I'll have to draft a pattern for him."

"You may as well," Katie said. "Hopefully, he'll be here forever."

She stepped into the workroom and quickly changed into the dress. It fit a little loose at the waist, but it was good enough.

She stared into the mirror. Her natural blonde hair was beginning to grow back beneath the brown, but the brown did seem to be more faded from when she first put it in.

She sighed, wondering how long she was going to have to live with two colors, but the only alternative was to chop off the brown an inch from her head. She wasn't ready for that.

She folded the blue dress and forced a smile as she stepped back out, handing it off. "Here. May the best Blackwell win."

Katherine grinned. "We should make a bet. I say Julie."

"Well, you would know better than me!" Katie teased.

Now that the garment was in her hand, Katherine explored the material, shaking her head. "I have no idea what this is made of. It falls very nicely, doesn't it? Oh, I see the staining on the back. I can probably get that out. What happened?"

"I got attacked by a young mountain lion. Neil pulled it off of me."

"And it didn't tear his face off?"

"No, Clark shot it."

"Everyone okay?"

"Mostly. Mallory was stitching up Neil's arm when we left. I think his heart was broken more than his body. He loves lions, and he's just figured out they're mean."

Katherine laughed sympathetically. "Poor man. What a start."

"Jeremy thinks he will adapt. I hope he's right."

"He'll have to. Sounds like he'll die if he doesn't."

Katie watched Katherine fold the dress, hesitating. Katherine was only three years older than herself. They'd gone to school together, closer friends than she'd been with Allison until Katherine turned fourteen and had left to work with her parents in her tailor shop. They'd bonded again, briefly, when Katherine's father died the same year Katie's had. But Allison was such a dominating friend, the quieter Katherine faded, except when the girls were alone. Katie wondered if that would change, now that they were all out of school.

Still. Katherine had nearly a decade of sewing experience by now and Katie could only embroider. She swallowed. "I need to find work," she said. "Mallory said I might ask here. I don't do a lot of sewing, but I could learn."

"Do you have the patience for it?" Katherine asked.

"I think I could find it," Katie ventured.

Katherine folded the dress and set it on the counter before she replied, "We could give it a try. I do need somebody. May as well be somebody I like. Besides you're better at math than me. You might be good with the measurements and drafting."

"I hadn't thought of that," Katie said. "Just worried about making straight stitches."

"That you'll have to learn," Katherine said. She eyed Katie's gown with a grimace. "But we could start by designing a dress that fits you better than that one does."

"It's good enough. I need it today." Katie gave Katherine a quick hug. "Thank you."

"Anytime," Katherine said. Her eyes sparkled. "Now tell me all about the city. Good. Bad. Everything."

Katie hesitated, countering with a request. "Why don't you plan on staying for dinner tonight when you come to measure Neil?"

"I will, thank you," Katherine answered. She paused before her eyes moved past Katie to the back door. "In fact, I have an idea."

"What?"

Katherine grinned. "I have to ask Jeremy."

The Gift

EVEN MALLORY, FOR ALL her skill in comforting, hadn't been able to keep Neil from fleeing to the hayloft. He sat with his bandaged arm wrapped around his knee, watching the wind rustle the trees. Katie grimaced as she stepped over the top of the ladder and sank next to him.

"My friend, Katherine, is coming today," she said. "She needs to measure you, so she can make you some clothes. Did you know you're the biggest guy in the town?"

Neil's eyebrows twitched, before he glanced sidelong at her.

"It's true," Katie said. "Most of the men are about Jeremy's height, though he says his dad was taller. Anyway, you'll like Katherine. She's calm. More like Mallory than me."

She trailed off because Neil wasn't listening. He was staring into the barnyard.

Katie twisted, then both winced and grinned as she caught sight of Jeremy and Mallory kissing near the pigpen. "Haven't you seen anyone kiss before?"

Neil shook his head.

Katie straightened. "Not even your parents?"

He sent her a baffled look and shook his head. Too startled to choose his words, he sputtered, "What...for?"

"That's what people do when they really like each other," Katie stammered. "I mean, when they want to get married and have a family and live together. And...I don't actually know why. It...it just feels nice."

The man's eyebrows twitched with his thoughts as his eyes roved the bits of hay on the floor. Katie swallowed, hoping he didn't try to kiss her and trying to think of something kind that would deter him.

"You can't just kiss anyone though," she said. "She has to want to kiss you back."

Neil blinked. His jawbone bulged before he said, "Like Clark?"

She sat stunned, but she replied, "Yes."

"I saw."

"You did?"

"I...didn't know...what you were doing."

Katie bit her lip. "I'm sorry I didn't tell you about Clark. I was scared to tell you, because I didn't think you'd let me leave if you knew. And then I didn't think you'd come with me. And I wanted you to come. I wanted you to have a home here like I do."

Neil's chin tightened. He pulled up his knees tighter, rubbing one with his uninjured thumb. "You broke my home."

"I know. I'm sorry." She shifted, turning toward him. "But you could make a new home. Easier than I can, honestly. You can buy just about any house here that you like. And you've got plenty of money to live on while you decide what kind of work you like to do. No one is going to shock you if you don't build worlds. You get to decide what you want to do."

He glanced back at her with somber eyes.

"And when you're ready, you can meet all the villagers," Katie said. "We do lots of things together. Sometimes we'll all work on building a new barn, sometimes we have weddings and dances, sometimes we go hunting, or out to collect mesquite pods. You can have a lot of friends, not just me. And, probably, someday you'll realize you want to kiss one of them, and she'll want to kiss you back."

"But not you."

"Not me," Katie answered.

Neil took a breath and his eyes returned to the barnyard, but Jeremy and Mallory had gone back to their chores. She braced herself, but then he asked, "What is...mesquite pod?"

Katie huffed a laugh and pointed through the window. "See that scraggly tree? That's a mesquite. They make seed pods in June, and we collect them. You can grind up the seeds to make a kind of bread. And alcohol."

"What's alcohol?"

"It's a drink. But don't drink too much of it, or you'll do dumb things and get sick."

He threw her an incredulous look. "Why drink?"

"It's just what some people do."

One side of his face scrunched before he shook his head. "Villagers are weird."

"Hallo!" Katherine's voice carried from the yard. She stood on the porch in a brown cloak.

Katie hung out of the hayloft to call. "We're up here!"

Katherine turned, grinned, and walked across the yard. Neil paled but made no protest beyond a swallow.

"She's bringing a surprise," Katie said before the man could flee. "She wouldn't even tell me what it is."

She was glad she'd invited Katherine to meet Neil before Allison's boisterous personality came along or they were confronted with any of the Blackwell glares. The girl represented an average villager: just a plain worker who made a steady living off sewing and friendly chitchat.

Katherine climbed the ladder, clutching one arm against her cloak like she was hiding something under it. Even though she'd been prepared for Neil's height, she still blinked in surprise when she saw him sitting next to Katie.

He watched her, warily, but with enough curiosity that Katie relaxed. "Neil, this is Katherine. Katherine, Neil."

"Hello, Neil." Katherine offered her hand.

Neil threw a panicked glance toward Katie.

Katherine's smile slipped, and she began to drop her hand, but Katie stood and said, "In our village, we shake hands like this."

She took Katherine's hand and gave it a shake, though their usual greeting had always been a quick hug.

Neil blinked. "Why?"

"I...don't know that either," Katie said, then laughed, looking toward Katherine. "Neil is making me rethink everything we do."

"It's just a way to show that you're willing to be friends," Katherine said. "That you're not going to hurt each other." She offered her hand again to the man.

He pushed himself to his feet, and Katherine kept her smile even when he towered over her. Her hand nearly disappeared inside of Neil's as he took it, and Katie hoped he didn't squeeze it too hard.

But he swallowed and found the best version of his voice to say, "Hello."

"Hi." Katherine's smile spread a bit. "Katie tells me you like lions."

Neil's eyes roamed from her, then back warily. "Yes."

"Have you ever seen a kitten?"

The man's face blanked as he released her hand. Thrown off, he only offered a mute headshake.

"They're like lions," Katherine said. She reached beneath her cloak and pulled out a wriggling orange kitten. "Little tiny lions."

"Katherine!" Katie gasped, the laughed. "Mallory is going to have words for you!"

Her friend grinned outright. "I asked Jeremy if I could give Neil a kitten. He said yes."

Katie snorted. "Oh, then Mallory is going to have words for him."

Neil's head tilted and traveled forward as he stared at the creature. He reached toward it, stroked the long hair with one finger. The corners of his mouth traveled up, higher than she'd ever seen them.

It had never occurred to Katie to get Neil a kitten, but it was a brilliant move on Katherine's part. The intrigue made Neil relax and the antics made Katherine laugh, and the three spent nearly an hour in the loft, vying for the pet's attention with bits of straw.

When Mallory called them for dinner, Katie hesitated, suddenly worried Neil would choose a cat over dinner. But she said, "Neil, we should leave it in a crate out here. Mallory won't like it in the house."

Neil's grin slipped. He eyed the kitten. But then his eyes flickered to Katherine as she stood and brushed the hay off. His eyes fell as he swallowed. But he rose without protest. As they neared the porch and the door, Katie felt his hand brush hers, but when she glanced down, he'd pulled his fingers into a trembling fist. His breath grew tighter as he climbed each of the wooden steps.

He watched while Mallory greeted Katherine with a hug instead of a handshake. When they cleared the door, he swayed back toward the barn. Katie pressed her lips together, waiting for him.

He glanced at her, took a breath, and stepped across the threshold.

The Confrontation

THE KITCHEN SEEMED dim now that Katie had gotten used to the lights of the city. Though the daylight still crept in from the windows, Jeremy had lit candles to stave off the shadows and built up the fire to drive away the chill.

Katherine asked a few questions about the city, but Katie steered the conversation onto local topics and her friend followed suit. The girls kept a steady stream of stories and gossip that highlighted the best of their village life.

Neil listened but kept himself busy poking at a green bean.

"That's what green beans look like when they're not microwaved to death," Katie teased.

"What's microwaved?" Mallory asked.

Neil snorted, glancing at Katie.

"It's what our bread box is supposed to do," Katie answered. "In the city, the buttons turn it on, and it heats up food in about a minute."

"How does it cook that fast without burning it?" Katherine asked.

"Magnetron makes...waves." Neil finally spoke, motioning with his hands. "Vibrates...molecules...but not air."

Katherine stared at him before she stammered, "I...didn't understand any of that."

Neil's smile vanished. His face flushed as he turned downward. "Sorry."

"Oh, I didn't mean that," Katherine said quickly. "I just...I've never heard some of those words. I don't know what they—"

Neil yelped, jolting in his chair so hard that the legs wobbles. His fork and knife clattered against the antique plate.

His fists clenched, but he quickly put his face into the crook of one elbow. He panted, leaking more voice into each breath.

Katherine and Katie had jumped too, but Katherine recovered more quickly, fear turning into concern. "Neil, are you okay?"

Anyone with eyes could see that he wasn't, but the question made him slowly pull himself up. His eyes were half filled with tears, bright with fear.

Jeremy stood, rounding the corner of the table. "What happened, what's wrong?"

"Jeremy, don't touch him." Katie had meant the warning to come stronger, but she only managed a hoarse whisper like she and Neil had exchanged vocal cords.

She sat stunned, mind working to find an explanation that didn't involve the truth. AIDA was dead, the village had no electricity at all. How had she shocked Neil?

"You said 'sorry,'" she stammered.

Neil's hand went to his throat.

She glanced toward him, but he was watching her, searching for an explanation. The fine lines in his face were arranging themselves into a mounting expression of terror.

"Katie, what's going on?" Mallory asked.

Even Jeremy looked to her for answers, but Katie could only shake her head. Neil had already said sorry many times, even reveled in repeating it over and over to prove that AIDA really was dead. Only now, suddenly, she wasn't, which had to mean she'd synced again with some sort of local source.

Her right ear picked up the hum of an unfamiliar engine. The back of her knees hit her chair, sending it into a wobble, then a crash as Katie ran to the door to slam it. "No, no, this can't be happening!"

"Katie?" Jeremy asked.

Her throat grew tighter with each second. She hadn't entirely ruled out that the Alcotts may come after them. But even if they came, she'd counted on meeting them, an entire village against two people in the outborder where the lack of electricity put them on equal footing.

She spun, slamming her back against the door to stare at Neil. "How is AIDA here? How is she here!"

"Who is AIDA?" Mallory stood, swaying first toward Katie, then toward the back door.

"AIDA shocks Neil. It's how the Alcotts control him," Katie said. "But she's...I don't..."

Something crashed into the back door before it burst open. Katie screamed, but it was Clark who rushed in. He'd lost his hat somewhere. His hair stuck in odd directions, waving above his head as he swiveled it around the room, finding Katie's eyes first, then Neil. "Go!" he hissed. "Go, they're looking for you."

Katie rushed to Neil, but the man sat frozen at the table. The front steps shook under several pairs of feet. Katie crawled beneath the tablecloth, motioning Neil to follow her. Katherine shoved his shoulders, and the man finally dropped to his knees, following Katie. From the other side, Mallory shoved a plate and glass beneath the tablecloth.

Katherine followed her lead with Katie's dinnerware and nearly knocked Neil's head with the sliding fork. It clattered on the wooden floor, but he grabbed the plate and glass, setting them beneath the table legs.

The door thundered beneath three hard knocks. This time, it was Neil who grabbed Katie to keep her from bolting out of hiding.

Katie curled to press her ear against the floor, peering beneath the edge of the tablecloth, just in time to see the lumps of caked mud fall from Jeremy's boots as he walked toward the door.

He stood and called through, "Who is it?"

"It's Mayor Blackwell!"

Katie's head began a slow swim.

Wood scraped against wood, and a puff of air shook the thin tablecloth as Jeremy opened the door.

Mallory's friendly tone was ruined by the rapid breath that punctuated her words. "Mr. Blackwell. We didn't expect to see you. Come in. How are you? Who is this?"

"Don't waste my time," Mr. Alcott answered. "I have come to collect my son and his property."

"Your...son?" Mallory's surprise added a reality to her act. "What..."

"We don't know anything about your son," Jeremy stated.

"Obviously." Mr. Alcott's voice rose. "If you did, you'd know that he has a tracker. Which means I can find him. Any time he runs. Anywhere he goes."

Katie lifted her head to stare at Neil, meeting his eyes, only inches away. They were glassy with a bright glint of despair.

Mrs. Blackwell spoke suddenly, though she sounded more anxious than stern. "So, we know he's here. If he is here, so is she. And if you bring them out right now, we can leave right away."

"If you don't, you'll be arrested," Mayor Blackwell said.

"Excuse me?" Jeremy's voice rose.

"What are you talking about?" Mallory asked. "Mr. Alcott, we don't have your son here. And as for Katie..."

Mr. Alcott sighed. "AIDA, engage in correction mode eight."

"Rich, please," Mrs. Alcott's voice rose in a squeak. "There's no need! Please! Please bring out Neil. We just want Neil, don't we, darling? We just want our son."

Time was such a strange thing. It stretched on in silence long enough for Katie to press her fingers hard into Neil's hand. For Neil's eyes to fall to the floor, for his face to pale, for him to caress his throat, for the lines in his face to sink downward. His eyes grew dulled like they had the first morning in the kitchen.

"AIDA," Mr. Alcott said.

Katie's eyes flooded, both tears dropping to the floor, instantly replaced.

Neil rolled toward the tablecloth, disappearing beneath. It fell like a curtain.

"Ah. There you are." Mr. Alcott's voice remained calculatedly cold. "Where's your girl? Is she down there with you?"

"No," Neil said.

"AIDA, correct Neil's lie."

Katie crawled out, but not fast enough to keep Neil from collapsing, clutching his throat, growling in a vain attempt to stifle his scream.

"What are you doing?" Jeremy stepped toward Neil, then whirled toward Mr. Alcott.

"I told you I am here to collect my son and Katie," Mr. Alcott said. His tone was cold, and his words were clear and clipped. "If you try to stop me, I will bring charges of theft against you."

"Theft? You kidnapped her!" Mallory said.

"I did not. I bought her."

"What?" Katie sputtered.

Clark strode across the room and seized Katie's hand. "That is a lie!"

"No, it's not," Mr. Alcott said. "I have the legal paperwork right here that states Katie belongs to me, and I gifted her to my son."

"What?" Clark yelled louder than Katie had ever heard him.

Mallory snatched the paper from the man's hands. "Katie was never for sale! You promised her a scholarship and tricked us into sending her!"

Mr. Alcott blinked, folding his arms as Mallory scanned the paper, pretending she could read its words.

Katie wobbled toward her sister, taking the paper. There was the date of her sister's marriage. There was Mr. Alcott's name in a careless signature. And there was Mayor Blackwell's name, right next to it.

"What is it?" Mallory panted. "What does it say?"

Her mouth fell as her face lifted toward the man who stood against the wall. "How could you?" Katie whispered before she yelled. "You had no right!"

Mr. Blackwell's nose rose as he stated, "As mayor, I have the legal authority to relocate my citizens in order to preserve resources. Katie wanted to go to the city. And if there was a wealthy family looking to provide a young lady with a good home, who promised to take care of her..."

"And we *did* take care of her!" Mrs. Alcott interjected. "We took very good care of her."

"You locked me in a house!" Katy cried.

Jeremy reached for the rifle over the door and racked it. "You are not taking Katie anywhere. I don't care who's mayor."

"Don't you dare threaten me!" Mayor Blackwell roared.

Clark snatched the papers from Katie's hand, crumbled them, and threw them into the fireplace. He shot his father a defiant look.

Mr. Alcott took a breath. "I can get another copy of that paper."

"I can get another bullet for this gun," Jeremy countered.

"Perhaps," Mrs. Alcott suggested in a very small voice, "we could get a refund?"

"How much?" Mallory asked.

"$5,000 UCs," Mr. Alcott said.

"Katie...is...mine," Neil rasped.

Jeremy glared. "Why don't you just take our mayor instead for an even trade?"

"Jeremy," Mayor Blackwell spoke. "Don't do anything stupid. We will let Mr. Alcott take Katie and Neil, and we will not stop him."

Clark pulled in a breath, turning toward Mr. Alcott. "I will buy Katie from you."

"You, son, don't have enough to buy Katie!" Mr. Blackwell roared.

"I'll get it," Clark snapped.

"From who?" Mr. Blackwell asked. "Not us."

"Katie is mine!" Neil roared. His voice rose above the rasp. It rang, commanding every eye in the room to swing toward him. He glared at his father, speaking distinctly. "She wants...to stay. She stays."

"Well, then it's all settled." Mrs. Alcott held out her arm, almost desperately. "Come home. We'll find you another girl."

The air left Neil's lungs like he'd been punched. He'd used up most of his voice, but he pushed out another sentence that came in a grating wobble. "I want to stay."

Mr. Alcott pressed his tongue against his teeth. "That's not an option."

"Of course it is," Mallory said. "He's a grown man. He's welcome to stay with us."

"Katie doesn't want you, Neil," Mr. Alcott spoke with slow, distinct words. "She lied to you. Everything she told you was just to trick you into helping her escape."

Neil's entire face changed from white to red, his chest freezing mid-breath.

"That's not true," Katie said.

"You had no intention of staying with Neil here," Mr. Alcott insisted. "You just used him to break you out and dragged him through the wilderness so you could get back to this guy."

He motioned toward Clark, who threw a surprised glance toward Katie.

She shook her head, sputtering, "I never...I said Neil could be free here, and he can be! He's Class A. He has no restrictions."

"See Neil?" Mr. Alcott said, "She doesn't want you! There's nothing for you here."

"That's not true!"

"How many times has she lied to you?"

Katie swung toward Neil. He'd ducked his head, closing his eyes, but the effort hadn't covered the shame that slumped his shoulders.

"Neil, I opened the door for you," Katie said. "I wouldn't have opened the door if I wanted you to stay behind."

"Well, which one do you want, Katie?" Mr. Alcott demanded. "Neil or this guy?"

"That's not fair!" Clark snapped.

Neil dropped his head so low she couldn't see his expression, only the rise and fall of his throat as he swallowed. "I don't...want Katie. I want...to stay."

Mr. Alcott dug his phone from his pocket, hit a button, and spoke into it. "AIDA, engage correction mode ten."

"Richard!" Mrs. Alcott screamed. "Take it off! Take it off right now!"

"Neil," Mr. Alcott spoke evenly. "You are coming home, with or without Katie. Now walk."

"Come on, darling." Mrs. Alcott held out her arms. "Please come. Please, baby, come."

Neil's face was hazy at it turned toward the window, where the evening sunlight fell into a square across the floor. Lit by the glow, his eyes shone with moisture before a blink cleared them. He looked at his parents. Lifted his chin and spoke distinctly. "I'm sorry."

The word stunned the room.

Mr. Alcott's eyes bulged. "AIDA, disengage!" The man shook where he stood, screaming louder. "Disengage!"

Neil shuddered.

Mr. Alcott dropped the phone. He charged toward his son, caught Neil's chest, let out a scream as the electricity locked their bodies together. The two bodies shook, both thrown as one unit against the wall. Mr. Alcott's head indented the whitewashed sheetrock with a loud crack. The jolting stopped. They slid apart, but Mr. Alcott landed first before Neil crumpled on top of him. A halo of blood pooled around the man's head.

Neil lay draped across the man, his forehead touching the wooden boards of the floor. He didn't move.

Katie screamed, wresting herself from Clark's grip.

Mrs. Alcott sagged, catching herself on the table before she collapsed onto her knees.

"Correction mode disengaged," AIDA announced.

Katie snatched the device from the floorboard. She slammed it against the wood, stamping it with her heel. Cracks spidered across the screen. She kicked it, sending it ricocheting against the wall where it split, spitting out the battery.

"Katie! Katie!" Clark lurched to catch her hand.

She pulled away from him, and her knees throbbed after they hit the boards. Sobbing, she gingerly touched Neil's chest. Found no current, no shock. No pulse.

"Clark, do something," Katie panted.

"I-I don't know what to do," Clark sputtered. "I don't even know what happened!"

"Lightning..." Katie sputtered. "It's like lightening!"

Clark blew out a breath, shook himself into focus. He rolled Neil to lay flat on the floor, felt for a pulse, then planted his palms on Neil's chest and pumped his weight onto the larger man, already shaking his head with doubt. "I don't think this will work."

"It'll work," Katie said. "It has to." She stared as Clark pinched Neil's nose and blew hard into his mouth, then pumped again. She crawled to Neil's head. "I'll blow. Tell me when to blow."

"Now," Clark said.

Neil's skin was red with burns. Katie put her mouth to his lips, refilling his lungs, then squeezing her eyes as Clark pumped again. She heard something crack. "What was that?"

"A rib. Keep going."

Katie sobbed but sucked in a breath and tried again.

Mr. Alcott's vacant gaze stared past her. His face looked like a mask frozen forever in pain.

"Neil, please. Please, please," Katie whispered as Clark put his full weight on the man's sternum.

"Katie... honey..." Mallory's voice carried softly like it did the day they buried their parents, and Katie wouldn't let them shut up the coffins.

"No!" Katie barked at her, then begged. "Clark. Don't stop. Please don't stop."

Clark panted, trying another three pumps and Katie blew. Over and over again until she was dizzy, until Mr. Alcott's blood had pooled around her knees, until Mrs. Alcott's sobs had turned into screams that even Mallory's hug couldn't muffle.

Until the lines in Neil's face twitched, rearranging themselves into a subtle expression that belied the pain beneath. His chest pumped three times. Then he took the tiniest sip of a breath.

Starting Again

One Year Later

Katie tugged the wrinkles from the white gown. She studied the hem, noting with satisfaction that her seam was nearly flawless. The lace gathered into a full-skirted drape that ruched the train, ready to be let out or taken in for the next bride. Most likely it would be let out; there were few girls in the town shorter than herself.

But—at least for today—the gown fit her. It had been the most nerve-racking project Katherine had forced her through, but she'd done well and had finished in time.

Katherine let herself into the sewing room, smiling at Katie. "That looks perfect."

"I still can't believe you made me sew the village wedding dress."

"I told you that you would do well, and you did," Katherine threw back before adding. "And just in case, I sewed one too."

Katie gasped, turning toward her. "You did not!"

"I told you I'd always have your back," Katherine said. "Besides, it'll be nice for a bride to have options."

"Well, can I see it? Maybe I want to choose it."

"You can't. It's too late for alterations. I knew you'd do just fine on yours, so I made it to fit me."

Katie swiveled her head, but Katherine had turned her back and was busy cutting out a pattern.

"Should I read into that story?" Katie teased.

"You can read whatever story you want," Katherine said. "And after your wedding, I'll tell you the real one."

"Katie!" The bell jingled on the front door. Allison's boots vibrated the floor as she sprinted into the room with a box in one hand and a letter in the other. "I hope you invited Mrs. Bonnie, because she asked me to bring you a hat."

Katie laughed. "We did invite her. In fact, we invited everyone in the village, including the former mayor. If the Blackwells don't come tonight, that's on them."

"Well, at least some of them are coming. The groom and his aunt."

"And cousin," Katherine said. "Julie Blackwell bought that city dress."

Katie giggled. "Did she really?"

"Well, I took it apart and made it into something new," Katherine answered. "I didn't want to remind Neil of you every time he saw it."

"I'm pretty sure Neil is over me," Katie said. She took the box lid off and felt her smile slip as she caught sight of the dried geraniums. "I hope Ms. Bonnie doesn't want me to wear this for the dance."

"Don't open it until after," Katherine advised. "Then you can play ignorant. It'll look great on you in your garden."

"Garden?" Katie asked.

Allison cocked her head. "Every bride starts a garden. How else are you going to feed your husband?"

Katie winced. "I guess he'll starve. I'm no good at gardening, and I'm always here."

"I have a garden, and I'm always here," Katherine countered.

"Yes, but you're superwoman."

"Cotton is in your blood. Gardening is only one step away."

It was also the chore she avoided the most, but Katie took a breath. "Will you at least help me plant it?"

"Of course we will," Allison said. She held out the envelope. "Tucker brought a card from town and asked me to give it to you."

"You can burn it," Katie said.

"You should open this one. It might have money."

"Why would it have money? I'm not marrying her son."

"Just in case." Allison slipped her finger under the flap and pulled the card free. She grinned and held up a universal currency card. "See?"

"Well, that will come in handy next time we visit the inborder," Katie countered sarcastically.

"If you don't want it, I'll keep it," Allison teased. Her eyes went to the card as she read in her best Mrs. Alcott voice. "Dearest Katie..."

"Ooh, you're dearest now," Katherine teased.

"Please accept my sincere congratulations on your marriage to Clark."

"She's keeping tabs on us," Katie muttered to Katherine.

"I am truly happy for you and would love a note to hear how you are doing when you get settled in. Please use this money to buy something nice for your new home. Mrs. Alcott."

She paused, and Katie added, "P.S. tell Neil..."

Allison held up her finger to cut her off before she grinned and read, "P.S. I have looked into a specialist out of Newpark that I believe can help Neil if he is still experiencing any setbacks with his health. Please tell Neil if he decides to meet with him, he may stay with me at our home."

"Uh, no," said Katherine.

Allison glanced at her, then grinned as she continued, "I will not lock the door. And he may bring his girl. I heard he found someone in the village." Her eyebrows tucked. "Who did she hear from?"

"Probably a Blackwell," Katie muttered.

"Careful," Katherine said. She placed the veil on the neck of the dress form and shook it out to relax the wrinkles. "You're about to become a Blackwell."

A knock came from the porch door and Allison called, "If you're Clark, you may not come in!"

Katherine grinned softly. "That's not Clark. That's Neil."

There was a spring to her step as she left to open the front door. Neil still hadn't learned which doors needed knocking and which he could just walk in, so he knocked at all of them.

Allison sighed softly. "I'd be jealous if I wasn't so happy for y'all."

"I think they are engaged," Katie said. "Katherine's acting funny, and Neil came home so excited last week, but he just shrugged off all our questions. It's hard to guess. He gets excited over the most random things."

"I know. He's funny." Allison chuckled. "He saw one of our chicks hatch the other day, and I thought it was going to give him a heart attack."

"I wondered why he quit eating eggs," Katie said.

Allison's bit her lip on a grin like she always did when she was contemplating telling a secret. Then she gave up and said, "Did you know he started talking?"

Katie stared. "Wait, you mean with words?"

Allison squealed and nodded. "He finally talked."

"Little stinker! He hasn't talked to me!"

"Well, it probably still hurts. And he hasn't talked to me either."

"Then how do you know he's talking?"

"Because Katherine said he told her good morning."

"She didn't tell me that! He hasn't said a word in over a year!"

"Well, I guess he found something worth saying."

"I guess so."

Katie turned back to the box, scolding herself for the flicker of jealousy. It wasn't much of a secret that Katherine and Neil had bonded over the last year.

She had spied a letter in the dress shop months ago, with the same neat handwriting that had once warned her about lions now writing something else for someone else.

But Neil had lived with them. At first, he'd recovered in the room that had been originally meant for her. Then he'd managed to climb the loft ladder again and had reclaimed the space for his own.

His skin had been burned all over but had slowly healed. His body, however, had stayed so weak that Clark was afraid his organs had sustained damage. His eyes had been sad, perhaps mourning the loss of Katie, perhaps working through the growing evidence that his parents had kept him inside, not to keep him safe as much as to keep his paycheck safely within their reach.

But Katherine had come, undaunted by his silence, first with aloe vera leaves to heal the burns, then with clothes that helped him blend in with the locals, and eventually with just a smile. It was everything Katie had hoped for, that Neil would find a place in the village and get the idea of creating a pride with her out of his head.

But it still stung a bit when it had taken a while for him to make eye contact with her, and no one had ever told him what had happened between the moments he called his father's bluff and woke back up on the floor, fighting to breathe again.

She shoved away all the thoughts. She was marrying Clark. She had to let go completely of responsibility for Neil and let him figure out his own future. She also cocked a knowing smile at Allison. "So, he just randomly said good morning and went back to silence?"

"He...might have managed a little bit more," Allison said, then quickly tacked on, "but not much. He said good morning and then asked her a question, and that's all he could manage before his voice gave out."

Katie's grin spread. "So he *did* ask her to marry him..."

"I didn't say that!"

Katie laughed and turned to put the hat back into the box and close the lid, so she didn't have to look at it anymore. "You're not denying it either."

Allison moaned. "Please don't tell Katherine that I told you. Act surprised when she does. She didn't want to take away any excitement from your wedding, but I suck at secrets."

Katie set the hat box on the shelf. "Well, I pretty much figured that one out on my own."

The two girls straightened as Katherine's quick step punctuated Neil's slower stride as the two crossed the main room again. Katie flashed a glance toward their hands, expecting them to be interlaced, but the pair must have decided ahead of time to keep their secret. Neil followed Katherine closely, then stepped to the side. His cat perched on his shoulder, already eyeing a spool of thread with a disconcerting amount of intrigue.

"Figured out what on your own?" Katherine asked.

"How to reuse part of the lace from the old dress," Katie answered while Allison flushed a deep red. "I like having something from Mallory's wedding. I'm also glad it's not the same dress."

"What about you, Neil?" Allison asked. "Do you like Katie's dress?"

Neil studied the cascading lace skirt and then the sleeveless bodice. Then he shook his head.

Allison gasped but Katie only snorted.

"Well, *I* like it," Katie said. "And that's all that matters." She eyed Katherine, suddenly more curious than ever about the second dress, adding coyly, "But it's good to know there's other options for future brides."

"Never ask Neil a question if you don't want a truthful answer," Katherine warned, ignoring the bait.

Neil flushed, but only offered a half-apologetic shrug. "I like Katie," he said.

His voice was soft, but clear. There was no rasp at all. Or any tone of regret. He actually smiled when the girls gasped.

"He is talking!" Allison squealed, and Katherine shot her a look.

The lines in Neil's eyes only lifted higher as Katie placed a hand over her heart. "Thanks, Neil. I think that's the best wedding gift I'm going to get. I like you too."

He sent her a nod but swallowed, apparently done for the day.

"Sure there's nothing else you want to tell us?" Katie eyed Neil, then Katherine but the girl had already turned to gather her bag.

"Katie, your wedding is tomorrow. All of your friends are keeping secrets. It's not nice to ask about them." She pressed the key into Katie's palm. "Lock up when you're ready. Neil and I have things to do."

"Well, be sure and take that cat with you," Katie threw back.

Neil sent her a frown and reached to comfort the animal who only sent her a lofty look.

Katherine laughed, reaching to scratch the cat's chin. "Sorry, Amari. You've been kicked out. Come on, Neil."

Neil gave the girls a wave and Katie returned it, feeling her smile slip as the trio disappeared. She sighed. "Everything changes again tomorrow, Allison."

"Oh, don't get mopey on me now," Allison said. "Neil's decided to talk again, and you and Clark are finally starting a life together. Katherine's all but officially engaged. *I'm* the one that should be moping."

"There's always Sam," Katie returned and only received a glare.

Allison sighed, then teased, "Do you want to walk home together? One last time before you're an old married woman stuck in your garden?"

"That garden seriously is going to need some help."

"Maybe Clark can barter an hour of labor with some of those people who never manage to pay him."

"That is not a bad idea," Katie said.

She and Clark would certainly never be wealthy. Even though Clark had lost his inheritance and distanced himself from his family, he still refused to sell any water. He hadn't the heart to charge fully for his services as a doctor, so there wasn't much coming in from that front either.

But it hadn't all been bad. Even now Clark was at their new house, finishing installing the well pump: their gift to the entire village, though they'd decided to wait a few days after the honeymoon to reveal it.

Katie left the workshop room, leaving her dress for the morning. She tucked Mrs. Alcott's currency card into her pocket as she walked through the shop. Better hang onto it, just in case. The bell tinkled as she closed the door.

Like the others in the village, she and Clark would join forces to combine their earnings and their elbow grease and create a decent life. It would be a happier life than any she and Neil would have managed locked in a house. And she suspected, it would even be a happier life than the one she may have found if she had gone to school and stayed in the city.

She was home now. And home was enough. She locked the door behind her and pocketed the key.

Don't miss out!

Visit the website below and you can sign up to receive emails whenever Lindsey Renée Backen publishes a new book. There's no charge and no obligation.

https://books2read.com/r/B-A-DRYJB-ZBLBF

Connecting independent readers to independent writers.

Also by Lindsey Renée Backen

Across the Distance
Swing
Between
Among
They Watch Us Like the Lions

Watch for more at www.everinkpress.com.

About the Author

Lindsey Renee Backen writes books that cross genres and themes: like life, their stories weave threads of the best and worst of moments, triumphs, and traumas. Her fiction is deeply character-driven, centered around the inner worlds of the characters as they face outer challenges, confront their flaws, and make sense of their worlds. In her books, you will find the innocence of first love, the trauma of war and family abuse, the struggle to break free of molds and expectations, and the complexity of family relationships. Not every character will get a fairytale ending, but read on, Friend. Lindsey believes that every story, whether in fiction or your life, can emerge from the darkest of places end in hope.

Read more at www.everinkpress.com.

About the Publisher

Read more at https://www.everinkpress.com.

www.ingramcontent.com/pod-product-compliance
Lightning Source LLC
Chambersburg PA
CBHW050347030726
47503CB00008B/2651